BOTTLE
in
AVALON

Neil S. Reddy

Illustrated by JP Lawrence

For Esme

Bottle in Avalon
Neil S. Reddy

ISBN 9780995475328
© Neil S. Reddy
Illustrations by JP Lawrence
First published by Dank House Manor 2014
Reviewed and corrected
Dank House Manor Publications 2024

Bottle
in
Avalon

The Good Folk Rule O.K!

(I Hate Faeries)

Foreword

I'm sure you've noticed there are lots of stories about fairies, in fact there seems to be an inexhaustible supply of books, plays, films and cartoons, packed with fairies or 'the Good Folk', as they prefer to be known. Many of these stories are beautiful and charming, sometimes even heart-warming and sweet.

And what's wrong with that? Well, it isn't accurate, you might even say they're complete and utter tosh - and that makes them dangerous. Dangerous how, I hear you say – what if you meet a real fairy? What are you going to do? Offer it your hand? Clap at it? Why not, they're only sweet, innocent little fairies. The original fairy tales were written for a reason, as a warning not to go into the woods alone, which is sensible advice, but what makes it such sensible advice? Here's one reason; in case you meet the Good Folk and get yourself eaten. Of course, you might be thinking, it's all make-believe anyway, what does it matter? Afterall that's why fairy stories are called fairy stories, nobody expects you to believe them, as it's all make-believe anyway. And in that case, have it your way, stop reading now, perhaps it's safer that way; but if you do carry on reading, know this, what I'm about to tell you is a true story, and I expect you to believe every word.

I confess certain details; some names, some places have been changed for the protection of the Good Folk, but everything else is just as I remember it.

Some minor details within the story do come directly from the Good Folk, so I can't vouch for those, because their idea of the truth is not our idea of the truth, and then there's the problem of sabotage and interference. I first published this story ten years ago, but those Good Folk just couldn't let it be and had to have their fun with the text; mixing up sentences and spellings and putting the ending where the beginning should be; the usual fairy mischief. Well this time, I've done my very best to make sure none of those interfering little tykes get their hands on this edition, but fairies are fairies, it's in their nature to play tricks, so realistically I can't promise there are no errors, but I promise this is as close to the truth as I can get...if there are any errors, if you find any... think fairy, and check the shadows.

There is only one thing you need to know before you start reading this story - fairies really don't like people. They never have and they never will, that doesn't make them bad or mean, it just means they're fairies, their ways are just not our ways. Anyhow enough of this, let's get going - my name is Kay, but you can call me Bottle.

BOTTLE
in
AVALON

My Dad was a milkman, and he loved his job. He said it was the best job in the world. He had a little speech, I'd heard it a hundred times, and it went like this;

"What a job, up early to see the best of the day and back home before everybody else even knows it's day! Best job in the world!"

Now that I've written that down, I realise my dad's cheerful outlook could be seen as rather annoying - how very odd it is to see that now - but I was young then, and of course I agreed with him; he was my dad.

I loved helping Dad out but could only do it on the weekends and school holidays. I would much rather have missed school and done the milk round. It really was good fun, driving around on a milk-float, delivering and collecting bottles, and I learnt how to do math too, collecting money, checking the change, and being paid tips; much more fun. Every Saturday I'd be there, riding the humming milk-float through the housing estate and out into the country lanes that surrounded the town. This was the best bit of the whole round. We'd regularly see foxes and badgers and even barn owls swooping through the trees. I loved my dad's milk round, except for the very last visit; Lone Farm. I hated Lone Farm.

There was something just plain wrong about it. Firstly, I never understood why a farm should need to have milk delivered, surely a farm had cows?

Every Saturday I'd say. "Shouldn't they have their own milk? A farm should have cows."

"Its arable land Kay, they grow barley and wheat. So no livestock."

"No cows..." that always bothered me, clear proof, or so I thought, that something was deeply wrong with Lone Farm - and I was right.

My story starts on a cold Easter weekend. The milk-float hummed, and the crates of empty bottles clinked behind us, as we made our way to our last delivery.

Have you ever been on a milk-float? Probably not, there's not many left these days; here's some things you need to know - they're not built for comfort or speed. They're battery powered, which back then meant they were pretty slow. There are no seat belts, and no real passenger seats, just a small padded wooden board set into the solid metal box of the cab, where the milkman is meant to carry his ledger, or maybe his breakfast. This means, if you were trying to sit on the wooden board, every pothole, bump and lump could jolt you right out of the cab.

The road to Lone Farm was as dipped and dented as it was possible for a road to be. Dad used to say the council didn't fix potholes, they moved them to Lone Farm Road, and it certainly felt that way. It was so bad, Dad had a job staying in his seat. He'd sit there gripping the steering wheel for dear life, with one foot braced against the door frame, pushing himself back into the seat, as the lumbering float dropped down into another divot.

I'd half stand, legs apart, next to him, bracing myself against the cab's roof. We called it road surfing; and we'd whoop and holler with every dip and drop; "Hang Ten!" my dad would say, and "here comes a big one," and "gnarly Dude!" in a truly awful American Surfer accent. I'd laugh from one end of that road to the other, until we rounded the bend, and the gates of Lone Farm came into view – that's when the fun stopped. Every time I saw that gate icy fingers scrapped down my spine. It gave me the willies, but I had a job to do; the last delivery of the day was always mine to make.

I jumped down from the cab, took the last two bottles from a crate and approached the gate. All the time scanning the long tree lined drive that led to the old farmhouse that sat hidden in the deep shadows. No matter how bright a morning it was, that darkness crouched there waiting for me, daring me to step into its lair – and I had to, I had no choice, there was money to collect.

I released the gate's metal latch, and as always it screeched like a frightened cat. I closed the gate behind me, and lent back against it so the latch fastened with a shriek – which is exactly what I wanted to do.

There were forty trees between the gate and the house. Twenty on each side. I know this because I counted them off as I passed each one. Eyes front never looking back, just in case something was sneaking up behind me.

At the third tree, a dense hedge of aggressive looking plants formed ranks on both sides of the path, creating a cold dark corridor filled with nothing but the sound of my feet on the gravel path, and whatever it was hissing at me from the hedge.

"Keep looking forward, keep going," I whispered to myself. I didn't look, I didn't dare, and I didn't need to; I knew something in the shadows was watching me.

Beneath the sixth tree on the right sat an old hen house with its roof collapsed in on itself, it was more cobweb than wood and as usual was swaying and groaning as if it was about to fall to pieces. I used to tread very carefully as I passed it, just in case my footsteps finally brought it crashing down, releasing ten thousand spiders, bent on revenge for breaking up their happy home. No thank you, tip toe, tip toe I went.

The seventh tree on the left wore a festering collar of used tyres. Thick tractor tyres, stubby worn car tyres and thin bicycles tyres. All draped in a slimy green moss, that buzzed with busy flies. It stank of stale water and something too sweet and rotten. I held my nose and hurried past, which brought me to the mouth of a yawning Yew tree, hollow and black at its centre, and all twisted around itself, as if frozen in a contorted scream.

The tenth tree was a large oak. It was so old and crooked I always kept my eyes on the branches as I hurried underneath. Just in case a branch broke off as I passed, or something reached down and tried to grab me. The thirteenth trees on both sides were full of wind-chimes made from old shells, boots, cups, mugs and broken garden forks. For the most part they remained perfectly silent until I drew near, and then they'd rattle like old bones despite the lack of any noticeable wind.

Under the next tree on the right, lay five or six toppled over bright orange gas containers, half covered with grass and weeds but still quite clearly set out in a rough triangle, as if someone had been playing skittles with them and had then grown bored of the game and never come back.

All of this I could deal with, counting the trees off as I went but the thing behind the seventeenth tree, it gives me the shivers to think of it to this day. It was a gigantic rusting bulk of a machine, half encased in a huge rotting wooden box, its centre had split open and out from it spilt cogs, wheels, lolling fan belts and twisted spikes on a swinging broken rotary drum. It looked like a gaping mouth with a set of bad teeth reaching out to bite whoever passed its way. I always tried not to look but on that Saturday morning, like every Saturday morning, I looked, and it looked back at me and grinned with hungry eyes. Run, run, run.

I forgot all about counting trees as I lost control of my feet and saw nothing but grasping shadows and heard nothing but howling trees, clattering bones and chattering teeth till I reached the giant black door of Lone Farm. Only then did I turn and look behind me – and there way-off down the drive was a patch of light where the milk-float sat waiting. It looked an awful long way away.

I put the milk bottles on the doorstep and leant against the door trying to catch my breath. The doorknocker was a big brass ring held in the mouth of a lion, I stared at it, and an odd feeling crept over me. Something was wrong or to be exact, missing. I couldn't figure out what it was, and then thought; "Where's the washbag?"

The farmer always left his milk money in an old tartan washbag; the kind of thing a man might keep his flannel and soap in when staying in hospital. The one I was looking for was greasy and smelt of old water and mushrooms. Every Saturday, without fail for the last three years, the stinky old bag had been there, but it wasn't there that morning.

I checked around the stone step, just in case it had fallen off and bounced away. It wasn't there but a foot or so away, in some blackened weeds, I found a full bottle of silver-top milk lying on its side. I picked it up and shook the bottle it hadn't separated or gone off yet, so it was probably yesterday's milk. Not a good sign, people don't forget to take their milk in, not for a whole day. I wondered if the farmer had gone on holiday and forgotten to tell us, but he hadn't been away once in the last three years I'd been doing the round. Something must have happened. I looked up at the great round doorknocker, its black cast-iron mane seemed to bristle with annoyance. I took its cold iron ring in my fingertips and knocked hard three times.

I counted to twenty, hoping all the time that the farmer would open the door and tell me off for disturbing him so early in the morning, but he didn't come so I knocked again. I suddenly felt very sick. I held the milk bottle high above my head and waved at the milk-float that seemed further away than ever.

Dad jumped off the float, launched himself over the gate and ran at top speed down the path. He took the bottle off me and shook it just as I had, and then he took hold of the doorknocker and brought it crashing down hard, three times. Nothing happened. Dad dropped to his knees and looked through the letterbox; his face grew pale. He looked at me; something bad had happened.

"Stay put son. I'm going to get some help. You stay here and I'll be right back."

"But Dad!" I protested because I really didn't like the idea of being left alone with whatever had happened beyond the farm's door.

"I'll be right back. Stay put," Dad insisted, already running back to the milk-float.

I watched as he drove down the road to where I knew an old telephone box sat – this happened in the days before networks and mobiles, so there was only one way to get help – calling from a phone box. The old dark house hunched over me like a giant. A giant with a horrible huge hammer wanting to squish me flat. I shut my eyes and refused to feel its hot breath on my neck. I thought about looking through that letterbox, but I knew if I did I'd see something I wouldn't be able to forget, so I sat there staring down the driveway, feeling the driveway staring back, longing to hear that friendly milk-float noise coming back up the road.

A brisk chill wind rolled up the drive, rustling the hedging and irritating the trees, as it worked its way to my face. I shut my eyes against the stinging blast, and sat there, shivering with the trees watching me and the rusty farm machines wanting to eat me up, and the old house wanting to fall down onto me, until suddenly the wind stopped, and I opened my eyes to see Dad jogging down the drive towards me.

"The police and an ambulance are on their way, we'd better stay, if you don't mind," Dad said as he jogged up to the house.

"Should we do something?"

"Just keep trying. Just in case." He dropped to his knees again and shouted through the letter box, "Hello, can you hear me? Hello there, the police are coming,"

Two policemen arrived and forced open the door. They walked in and moments later one of them returned and told Dad an ambulance would not be needed.

While a policeman wrote down what Dad told him, I sat in the shadow of the old farmhouse, looking up at it, thinking how sad it seemed now – the old farmer whose name I didn't even know had died alone in this dark old house and nobody knew until his milk money was due. It was the loneliest thing I'd ever heard. Didn't he have any family to care for him? Why was he all alone? What would happen to this sad old house now, would anybody ever look through those big old windows again? I looked up into those big empty glass eyes and for a moment I saw something, something tiny, green and very fast flit across the window. I didn't really know what I'd seen… but at the same time I did, I knew, I'd just seen a fairy.

Chapter 2

I remember that night very well, there was no way I was going to sleep, that strange fleeting glimpse had filled my head with tumbling questions. The only thing I knew about fairies was Peter Pan's Tinkerbell, and the thing I'd seen that morning looked nothing like her.

Seeing a fairy, surely it was impossible? It was much more likely to be a trick of the light. A reflection of a passing bird or perhaps a rat behind the dirty window, possibly a mouse, probably a rat? I didn't believe it, couldn't believe it, I'd seen a fairy with my own eyes. Before the sun had risen, I'd made up my mind, I was going back to Lone Farm.

Milkmen get up early, very early six days a week and therefore sleep very late on their one day off. Since Mum had been ill – I'll tell you more about that later - Dad liked to have me out of the house or as quiet as a mouse on Sunday mornings and being out was always easier than being quiet. So not only did I have the opportunity, I had permission to be out and about as early as I liked. Forget breakfast, I was dressed and out before the streetlights knew it was day.

By the time I reached Lone Farm, it was just getting light but not enough to touch the darkness that possessed that long lonely drive. I sat on the five-bar gate and looked into the gloom, my heart beating loudly; there was only one way I was going to make it all the way to the farmhouse.

I jumped off the gate and ran as fast as I could. Past the spooky trees and the wicked machines, past the rotting tyres, and the rattling nightmares. Run, run, run! I ran, ran, ran! All the way to the front door. I arrived panting, sick and dizzy – but I got there. I pushed hard against the door and of course it was locked. I stepped back onto the gravel drive and called up to the huge upstairs windows.

"Hello! Hello up there… I don't want to hurt you… hello can you hear me?"

There was no reply. I stuffed my hands into my pockets and waited but nothing happened. I'd come an awful long way on a Sunday morning for nothing to happen, so I picked up a stone and threw it at the house, it dinged off a window, and still nothing happened.

"I know you're in there. I saw you!" More nothing happened. "Right then…well I'm off then!" I shouted and turned to go.

A metal latch clicked behind me. I turned and saw the front door opening. I stood looking at the open door, and the deep dark emptiness beyond it.

"Hello?" I stepped towards the door, and it slammed shut. I stepped back and the door opened wide. I tried again – and so did the door.

"If you don't want me to come in, all you have to do is stay shut," I pointed out, "and I'll go."

Silence, I stepped forward and this time, the door stayed open. I took another step and then another and before I knew it, I was on the doorstep. I put my foot inside, leaned in as far as I could, and looked behind the door. There was nothing there. I took a big breath and stepped inside and then turned to watch the door close slowly behind me.

I was standing in a long narrow corridor with five doors leading off from it; two on either side and one in front. To my right was an old umbrella stand, it was crammed tight with tatty looking umbrellas and walking sticks, most with carved animal heads. I liked the look of one that had a carved head of a dog, I gripped it tightly and managed to work it out from the others. It had a good weight. I held it up like a club against my chest and instantly felt braver.

"Hello… is there somebody there?" I corrected myself, "is there something there?"

I heard a giggle and the door at the far end of the corridor clicked open. The giggling grew louder and then was hushed into silence. I raised the walking stick a little higher and held it a little tighter and walked through the door.

The room was empty, apart from the complete mess that filled it. It had clearly once been a kitchen and now was just a wrecked kitchen. All the cupboards were still there but there was no cooker, instead in the centre of the room was a campfire. Above which hung a large metal caldron on a twisted wooden tripod. The ceiling and the roof directly above the fire had been cut away to let the smoke out, but it couldn't work very well as everything was covered in soot and a thin layer of ash. Sooty cups, mugs, plates, pots and pans, some of which had things growing in them, covered every surface. Nobody had washed up for a very long time. A small circle of wooden chairs and several roughly made stools were gathered around the fire; between each were neatly stacked sawn logs and untidy piles of tinder sticks. In fact the room was dominated by wood, a tree had even pushed its way through a window and was trying to reach the hole in the ceiling, and the floor was covered with rotting pine tree branches. It looked as if someone had tried to move the outdoors indoors, and on the whole had done a pretty good job of it – but whoever they were, whoever had giggled and whoever had hushed them, was no-longer there.

"Where are they…?" I asked myself, squeezing the walking stick for comfort.

"If you squeeze any tighter, I'll be sick!" the walking stick in my hand shouted. It took off its wooden dog head and frowned at me.

I threw it across the room, jumped backwards and fell over a pile of logs. I lay there in a panic with my mouth full of pine needles.

The walking stick huffed and grumbled, then split its shaft into two long spindly legs, and kicked itself upright and strode towards me.

"Clumsy," it said, rattling with anger, "is that your name clumsy? If it isn't, it should be."

"Sorry," was all I could splutter.

"I dare say," it said, "a precious lot of good that does me. Nasty, hot sweaty human hands. Urgh! Horrible!"

"Go easy on the child Fiddle, you've had your fun. Did you bruise yourself child?" a voice like creaking ice interjected, "dinner is never the same once it's been bruised."

I jumped up, "No! Don't eat me!" I shouted, trying to see where the icy voice had come from, but seeing nothing but rubbish and a talking walking stick.

"But I'm hungry?" the voice creaked.

"I want the ears," said the walking stick.

"No please!" I cried and ran for the door. A steely hand gripped my shoulder, swung me around and lifted me off the floor. I was looking into a pair of diamond white eyes set into a face so pale it was blue.

"Not much meat," it crackled as it poked me in the ribs.

"Please don't eat me! I didn't mean any harm. I just needed to know, I saw you yesterday and needed to know. I'll do whatever you want but please don't eat me," I pleaded.

"It wants to trade," the blue face sneered, "but I'm very hungry. Your offer had better be good if I'm to forgo a meal," his metal grip tightened, "what is your life worth child?"

"I don't know."

"You'll sell yourself cheaply then. I offer you a pact. I demand silence as your pledge. Keep your silence and live. Talk and we shall feast on your bones. Agreed."

"Yes! Yes!" I cried, "I won't tell. I promise I won't, I just wanted…"

"Be quiet," it hissed, and then dropped me to the floor, "now then, let me look at you."

The thing stretched out across two rickety chairs and stared at me, looking me up and down. I was staring too but the difference was, I couldn't look away because I was terrified. It clearly wasn't. I was blinking tears from my eyes, but it wasn't blinking, because it didn't have any eyelids to blink. The thing, which I took to be male, was tall and thin, wrapped in a pale green cloak, beneath which he seemed to be wearing an even paler woven robe that looked as if it was made from dirty cobwebs. His face was hard and sharp, a collection of triangles covered in taut blue-white skin, but his eyes, those cold ice eyes were the worst; unblinking, constantly staring, sucking out the light that surrounded him. I just couldn't look away.

"For our part,' the thing said, addressing the room, "we promise you safe passage to and from this place and all the benefits therein. Your service to us will be rewarded, any treachery will be punished, severely. Do you understand?"

I nodded.

"Very well… bring out the contract!"

The room cheered, as from every corner and shadow, behind every teacup, through wall and ceiling came strange wild looking creatures of a hundred different shapes and sizes. Some were tiny, some nothing but smoke, others were as tall as they were round. Some were long and as twisted as rope, others smooth and glimmering, whilst many were as dirty as mud. In an instant the room was packed, and I was squeezed up against the chair where the cold-eyed creature rested his feet. A piece of grey slate as long as my arm was handed to the creature – he pointed to it with a thorn sharp bright blue fingernail.

"Name!" he demanded.

"Kay."

The whole room grumbled.

"Kay won't do. Kay was always a bully," he said.

"I am not!"

"Not you, the Pendragon's Kay. He was always a bully. No, that name won't do, it's taken, choose another!"

"Another name? I don't have another name?"

"What is your father's trade?" he sneered.

"Trade? He's a milkman."

"And your mother's a milkmaid no doubt."

At that everybody laughed…everybody except me.

I've mentioned that my Mum wasn't well, she wasn't well at all, and hearing people talk about her upset me. Hearing this blue-faced thing mock her was just too much. I just couldn't help myself. I jumped up and took a huge swing at him. He grabbed my hand in mid-flight and with one smooth gesture had me bent backwards with my hand behind my back, forcing me to my knees.

"Was that a challenge human? Luckily for you, I don't fight babes who've just left their wet-nurse's arms. You're no squire; you're probably not even good enough to be a villain."

The walking stick tapped itself on the ground, and insisted, "they don't have villains anymore, so he can't very well be one, because they don't have them anyhow."

"Perhaps not, but they're all villains, with nasty little tempers. Every last one of them. So, milksop, given your heritage, lineage and attitude, from henceforth you shall be called…Bottle," he pushed me away and I fell to the floor.

"Now for the legal documents, by the powers invested in me by the Crone Mother Morgana, and standing in the stead of the Green Man King, I declare this contract, binding…"

His long blue nail dug into the slate, which screeched and sparked in response. Every tooth in my head shuddered and every weird voice in the room moaned, shrieked and shivered along with me. I covered my ears and watched his nail curve and loop, as it cut strange swirling symbols into the screaming slate.

"Nearly done," the creature licked his nail and started writing again.

My teeth felt as if they were going to crumble at the sound.

Screech! "Nearly there…"

"Please stop!" I shouted.

Screech! "Nearly there…bit more…done,' he then spat on the slate, "all those without blood will seal the contract in the usual manner."

The slate was passed from creature to creature, and each spat in turn, loudly, fully and thickly onto the slate. Gross - and then it was handed to me. I was about to spit when the ice-skinned creature put his hand over my mouth.

"No Bottle, you must eat our words to fulfill the contract.'

I looked at the slate. "I can't eat that. I'll break my teeth."

"Fool. Eat our words not the slate."

"What?"

"Lick it."

"What? I can't do that, that's disgusting!"

"You must… or our contract is void."

"I can't!" I protested, "it's covered in spit."

"Shall we light the fire and boil the cauldron then?"

"I can't do it,' I insisted.

'Very well then…" he grabbed me by the neck and sank his long sharp nail into my arm. I yelped and tried to pull away, but he held me tight and pulled his bloody nail from my arm. He wrote 'Bottle' in large letters on the slate. He then pierced his own arm and wrote the word 'Thorn' in pale green blood beneath my name. "The spell is complete! You shall know them, as they shall know you when seen," Thorn declared, "Bottle of the contract."

Every strange face was smiling at me, and I knew their names. All their names. There was Pip, a tiny insect man the size and colour of a lacewing; there was Turnip and Tatty who resembled root vegetables. Sparrow, Lark and Jenny Wren and the Tit sisters Coal, Blue, Great and Long-Tail all of which reminded you of their bird namesakes but were clearly all tiny little girls. Willow, Sage, Comfrey and Briar, Hogweed, Balm and Russet – I knew them all.

"It is a simple magic," Thorn sneered, "and now being human as you are, there are bound to be questions, you are free to speak."

Every creature in the room sat down or hung in mid-air – whichever they found most comfortable – and began snoring.

"They have short attention spans," Thorn said as he scratched his nose, "and they know what you're going to ask before you ask it, we have been through this before."

"Well in that case perhaps I won't ask anything!" I snapped.

"Of course you will, you're bursting with questions, it's in your nature, and it can't be helped."

"Alright then," I said, thinking hard, "are you all fairies?"

The whole room groaned.

Thorn yawned, revealing a set of very sharp teeth in his bright blue mouth, "the word fairy is not a word we approve of, it's a human word."

"And faery isn't much better, its French," a small squat creature called Stone declared with some spite in his voice.

"Indeed," said Thorn," and we are of the Hollow Hills, of the Mystique Isle, the Isle of Mist, the last of Avalon in Albion. We were once called Elves or the Old Ones. Different invaders, Romans, Saxons and those Normans brought different words. They categorised us as they had the beasts of the field…and now we are the stuff of picture books."

"I thought you were… made-up too," I confessed.

"I don't believe in fairies!" the walking stick, called Fiddle, shouted out, "I don't believe in fairies! I don't believe in fairies!" Instantly every creature in the room began choking and writhing about in pain, and then, they all collapsed, falling to the ground, where they lay silent and still. I had no idea what had just happened – had I killed the fairies?

"I do believe in fairies!" Fiddle jumped up and cried, "I do, I do, I do believe in fairies!"

The room burst into laughter and applause, whilst Fiddle stood and took a bow.

"Understand this, Bottle," Thorn went on, "we are many, but we are one. We are not as you are or how you would like us to be. We are as we are, and we are true to nothing else. Your ways are not our ways."

Thorn's speech brought a ripple of applause and then all returned to their snoring; their attention spans really were appalling.

I thought hard, 'you all seem to have animal of plant names? Names made by men..."

"Or vice versa," Mud, the dirtiest creature in the room asserted.

"Well said," chirped Linnet.

"We are part of nature and are happy with our place in it, unlike man," Thorn hissed, "some have changed our names several times as the naming of nature has changed, as we prefer to use words in common usage..."

"Not all of us," Wythering Grass observed.

"Indeed, but we all refuse to use the Latin" Thorn said gravely, "we are all very old and we do hold grudges."

"We don't do the Latin," Fiddle insisted.

"I see, but what do you call yourselves? What should I call you?"

"The Good Folk has its charms," Thorn sighed, "mostly because it's wrong. It amuses us. Next question."

The next smart question, was the smart question; What did they want from me? If they weren't good or like the fairies from story books, what could they want with me? I decided that question was so important that I didn't want to hear the answer, so there was only one question left to ask; "Can I go?"

"If you want to."

"You won't try to stop me?"

"No. Why should we?" Thorn leant forward until his nose was almost touching mine, "we have signed a contract… and you have seen fairies, you'll be back, you couldn't keep away even if you wanted to."

I nodded, "I'll go then…if that's alright."

Thorn waved me away dismissively.

Half-hearted calls of "Bye, Bottle," and "Farewell Bottle," were mumbled, followed by a swell of snoring.

I stepped towards the door; no-one else moved. I stepped over Thistle and Giant Hogweed, and then stepped around Ripple and Dusk who were wrapped in each-other's wings, and finally I squeezed behind the snoring bulk of Hill and saw that his oversized behind was blocking the door. I couldn't open it more than two inches. I took the door in both hands, and using all my strength pushed it into Hill's bottom, but Hill's bottom held firm, not even a ripple. I put my foot against the wall and tried again, pushing with all my might. Hill farted; a long low rumble I felt through the floor, and then grunted and wriggled an inch forward. My eyes stung – it felt like my eyelashes were burning. But I held my breath and forced myself through the gap. And then I ran as fast as I could out of the house. I was halfway down the drive before I remembered to breathe. I was getting away as fast as I could. As I reached the five-bar gate a shape stepped out of the shadows, blocking my path, it was the long-legged Fiddle.

"In a hurry Bottle?" he grinned sourly with his wooden mouth, "would you mind picking these things up for us?" he handed me a piece of paper, "this should cover it, and keep the change." He grinned again and stepped back into the shadows. I stood there, frozen to the spot, listening to his high dry laugh disappearing off into the darkness of the trees.

I looked at what I'd been given. A role of crisp new banknotes and a long list of groceries, and then I knew what the Good Folk wanted from me, they wanted me to do their shopping.

Chapter 3

Pocket money was always a bit hit and miss in our house. It wasn't that my parents forgot to give it, but Mum hadn't been able to work for a while and money was tight, so Dad didn't always have it to give. So being given three hundred pounds in twenty-pound notes was a big deal. I could have got an awful lot of sweets for three hundred quid! But the temptation to spend the money wasn't the real problem, the problem was, where to hide it until the shops opened? It was the Easter weekend, and, in those days, shops didn't open on Sundays or Bank Holidays, which meant, I had to keep it hidden till they opened on Tuesday. If Dad found it, they'd be too many questions to answer, so I gave it a lot of thought - I decided, the best place was inside a bright green sock with pink stripes. One of my mum's, a present from Dad, but she wasn't going to be asking for them anytime soon.

Easter Monday was a busy day. Dad and I went to visit Mum, she'd gone into hospital for a rest, well that's what Dad said, but I knew more than he thought.

I knew the difference between a hospice and a hospital. People get better in hospitals, and Mum wasn't in a hospital. Dad was just trying to protect me, grown-ups tend to do that, when they think children can't handle the truth. What they do is keep quiet which is just hiding the truth, or they tell them something untrue, which is lying. Neither approach helps, it just makes the whole thing worse.

I wasn't new to the approach; the first time Mum went into hospital she called it a 'minor operation.' I didn't believe it then either. At least they'd be no more operations at the hospice, I knew that much. The visit didn't go so well, Mum hadn't slept the night before and looked thinner, frailer and more dried up than ever. She tried to chat but after ten minutes or so she fell asleep. We left about an hour later. Dad said we'd pop back that evening, but I don't think we did.

Being at home gave me plenty of time to catch up on homework, which I didn't do, but that's what Dad thought I was doing. I had more important things to think about, I had to make a plan. How was I to do the fairy's shopping? How would I get their shopping back to the farm? What if someone saw me? What would I tell Dad if he found out? I can't say I slept well that night either. My head didn't know what to worry about first, Mum, shopping, fairies. In the end, it all just got jumbled up into a big stew of weird dreams, full of hospital beds and sharp-nosed fairies with no eyes that chased me down endless rows of giant cornflake packets, whilst nurses dressed as milk bottles, smiled their dumb smiles and my father's milk-float sailed the high seas. I'm surprised my brain didn't just turn into soup and explode all over the walls.

Tuesday morning came and being Easter there was no school, so I got up with Dad to do the milk round. We worked our way steadily through the estate, with both of us running the deliveries, as we didn't have money to collect, we made good time which pleased Dad, then, just before we swung off down the country roads, I jumped off the float.

"Where you going?" Dad asked.

"I want to walk back. Is that alright?"

"Why?"

"I just got an idea for my homework."

"Remembered you haven't done it more like," Dad laughed.

"Maybe."

"Off you go then. Take care, don't talk to strangers, don't eat gravel. See you later gator," Dad grinned his silly grin and waved like a King to his people, as he drove his Royal milk-float away.

I'd got off the float to be near the new superstore they'd built on the edge of the estate. Superstores were very new things back then, and going there alone felt like a big deal, especially with so much money in my pocket.

I grabbed a trolley and began to shop. Now the shopping list the Good Folk had given me was certainly memorable, I'm sure I can recall most of it even today. Let's see:

1) 9 tins of biscuits

2) 10 family sized bags of crisps

3) 12 large bars of chocolate

4) 30 doughnuts

5) 6 bottles of fizzy pop of assorted flavours – I can't remember which.

6) 8 large bags of boiled sweets

7) 22 blocks of jelly

8) 40 Easter eggs

9) 3 bags of apples

10) 5 large bags of raisins… and a bag of spinach; a note at the end of the list read, "Don't forget the spinach," I guess they needed something green after all those sweets.

There I was throwing forty Easter eggs into the shopping trolley when I heard a cough behind me.

Standing there, with his arms crossed and a face like soured milk was a very large security guard. I could tell by the look in his eye that he didn't like the look of me at all. I guess he'd never seen a child with a shopping trolley full of Easter eggs and one bag of spinach.

"What are you up to?" he snarled.

"Shopping," I said.

"You got money for all that have you?"

I nodded, "Nearly done," I said, counting off the last of the Easter eggs, "thirty-seven, thirty-eight, thirty-nine and forty."

"You can pack that in right now!"

Suddenly there was a scream, followed by lots of shouting. The security guard pointed at me, and shouted, "You stay there!" and then ran off down the aisle.

There was more yelling and a scream and then an apple flew over the shelves and hit me on the head. An apple with a huge bite taken from it. I had to see where it came from, so I left the trolley and ran to join the gathered crowd at the fruit and veg aisle.

A very old, incredibly skinny old man with a long beard and wild hair; wearing nothing but tight leather shorts was searching through the trays of apples as if his life depended on it. He'd grab an apple, sniff it and then throw it to the floor, or at the security guard, who was now trying to stop him chucking around the apples.

"You owe me the last! You owe me the last! Where is she? You have hidden her from me!" the old man was shouting.

Another security guard arrived and together the two sweaty men overpowered the old man and dragged him away. That was rather upsetting to see, I didn't like that at all. But the strangest thing was, I was sure I knew the old man, but couldn't think of a name and I couldn't think how I could possibly know him, as I was equally sure I'd never seen him before. The crowd dispersed and I came to my senses and remembered my trolley. If the security guard was busy, it was time to make good my escape. I pushed the trolley at top speed to the checkout tills.

"On your own today dear?" the permed lady behind the till asked sweetly. I nodded. "Somebodies got a party planned, haven't they?" she said with a grin. I nodded again. "Want some help with the packing dear?"

"Yes please," I replied.

"Now before we start. You do have the money to pay, don't you dear? Would you mind showing me?"

She thought I was playing shops! Just some kid messing around, making trouble. I didn't like that very much, but I really enjoyed pulling out the roll of money and putting it under her nose.

"That's a lot of money to be carrying around darling. You put it away now and keep it safe, I'll help you pack."

The rest was easy. I loaded up the trolley, pushed it to the entrance, where there were three pay phones, covered with taxi company stickers. I phoned one, and ten minutes later it turned up. Once again, I had to show the driver - a skinny man with a shiny head and bright blonde eyebrows – that I had money before he'd agree to take me, but once that was done, he was happy to drive me down Lone Farm's crazy bumpy road. He even helped me unload the shopping at the gate. I paid him and off he went. I'd done it! The fairy's task had been completed. I'd never felt so proud.

As soon as the taxi was out of sight, Fiddle, Hill and a small untidy looking creature called Scrub, stepped out of the trees.

"Back again then," said Fiddle, not even trying to hide the surprise in his voice, "and you got the stuff. Good, took your time though. I thought we were going to have to come and get you."

"Here's the change," I handed it to him, "one hundred and ten pounds, forty two pence," I said.

Fiddle gave me his thin wooden smile, "I told you to keep the change."

"I don't want it," I heard myself say.

"Then throw it away child, it's of no use to me," and with that the creatures picked up all the bags of shopping, and loaded them onto Hill's back. I stood there watching Hill and the Good Folk walking down the drive, not sure what to do next. I put the money back into my pocket and turned to go.

"Bottle!" Fiddle shouted, "only you can choose to follow."

I jumped over the gate and ran down the path to join them.

"Now listen, Bottle," said Fiddle firmly, "these are ancient laws that must never be broken. Never accept food from us. Never eat anything in Avalon, and never eat anything from Avalon. That which belongs to Avalon stays in Avalon and that which is of Avalon, is always Avalon. Do I make myself clear?"

"Not really."

"Do you understand?"

"Never eat and never take anything from Avalon, and where Avalon is… is Avalon. But…' I just had to ask, "what is Avalon?"

Fiddle sniffed and shook his head as best he could, seeing as how he didn't have a neck.

Chapter 4

The kitchen was much as I'd first seen it, empty of creatures; a disorganized outdoor campsite indoors.

"Put the bags anywhere," said Fiddle dropping them where he stood, "right follow me." He said striding through a door in the kitchen's far wall. A door I'm sure hadn't been there the day before. I followed and found myself outside in the backyard of the farmhouse, except there was no yard – Fiddle must have been waiting for the look of shock that covered my face, because he spread his knitting needle arms wide and declared, 'Avalon!'

Forty feet from where I stood was a swirling veil of mist, with a hint of more solid shapes within it, but in front of me, right in front of me, just two steps beyond where I stood, was nothing. A cavernous gap, that dropped down further than I dared to look down; then a hint of a white cliff face beyond it and then that shifting mist.

To my right was an old wooden barn, painted red and looking decidedly shaky, like a sneeze could bring it down, and just to my left, was the oldest, rottenest, rickety wooden bridge – without handrails – I had ever seen. It was fourteen yards long, barely enough to cross the chasm - and only two foot wide. The far end seemed to be tied to something solid hidden in the mist but at my end, four large metal tent pegs seemed to be the only things holding it in place.

I knew nothing about bridges, but I knew that was one very dodgy looking bridge.

"Watch your step, it's slippery," Fiddle shouted, as he sped across the bridge, "it's easier if you don't think," he added as he looked down into the chasm from the other side, "oh doesn't bear thinking about… go on then get on with it."

"Me," I said, looking at the rotten planks, "no way! I'm not doing that."

"Come on, come on, get on with it Bottle. Come on, come on, before Pendragon wakes," Fiddle clicked his long wooden fingers together as if he were calling to a dog.

I put one foot on to the bridge and felt it give slightly underneath my weight and stepped off.

"Come on, get on with it!" said Fiddle turning his back on me and yawning.

I tried again, and again the bridge shifted slightly but I kept going. I took another step and it swayed and creaked in protest, and then my knees started quaking, making the bridge violently tremble and shiver, but I couldn't stop them doing it. I looked down and saw a bird flying way below me and at the bottom, in the grey distance, a pencil thin river that began to shimmer and shake faster and faster as the bridge began to shake itself to bits!

I knew I wasn't going to make it across! I couldn't turn round, I couldn't move, my legs wouldn't let me! I was stuck and at any moment the bridge was going to fall apart, and I was going to topple off and see how far the fall was!

"Oi! Come on Bottle, stop messing about!" came a shrill high voice from behind me, followed by a sharp jab of pain in my backside that made me jump, and suddenly I was skipping along the bridge! One, two and three and then my knees buckled, and I was falling. Luckily, I fell face down on the other side of the bridge. I sat there rubbing my nose and my aching stinging bum.

A short bushy creature with bright green skin was ambling across the bridge towards me, it was Nettle, who sure enough was covered with sharp green nettles. He rubbed his nose as he stood over me.

"Sorry for sticking my nose in where it's not wanted," he smiled. "I would help you up, but you wouldn't thank me," he said showing me his spiky green hands.

"I appreciate your help,' I nodded, although my bum was stinging something rotten.

"You want to find Dock and get her to rub that for you," he said with confidence, "she wouldn't mind. Just call her Doctor Dock, she loves that. Doctor Dock, who's there? Doctor, Doctor Who, no Doctor Dock – that was the old farmers favorite joke, that was. No idea why.'"

"Where are you going on about Nettle?" Fiddle asked irritably.

"I have no idea." Nettle replied.

"Right then, take Bottle with you because I'm staying here. That bridge has quite worn me out."

"Worn you out!" I blurted in utter disbelief, "for a walking stick, you really don't like walking very much do you?"

Fiddle jumped up, "You try it for two hundred years and see how you like it. I'll have you know I used to be a Silver Birch. I never asked to be a walking stick! It's you and your crafty crafting kind that did this to me! Can't leave well enough alone can you, humans!" he shouted and in a fit of pique ran back across the bridge and disappeared into the house.

"I didn't mean to upset him," I said.

"Don't mind him. He's a liar anyhow, we all know he asked to be made into a walking stick. When he was a tree, he used to moan on and on about not going anywhere, and then he gets what he wanted, and now listen to him. Let that be a lesson to you Bottle, be careful what you wish for," Nettle said thoughtfully as he pulled a plump caterpillar out of his hair, "want a look around then?"

"Please," I said.

"Pleasure, I can't say I've looked for a long time myself, too busy, I can't remember what I've been doing exactly but it must have been busy to stop me remembering, don't you think…. Not sure if I do. Now what were we doing?" he said as he flicked the caterpillar into his mouth, "Show him Avalon, that's it! Now, no holding hands," he chuckled and set off into the mist, "let's go see what all the fuss was about."

I would have been daft not to follow. My first sight of Avalon, how to describe it? Imagine a light mist rising in front of you and as it melts away it reveals a circle of enormous standing stones, old and grey but covered with bright coloured lichen and deep moss, and through them, you can see a valley that just shouldn't be there. It's long and thin and packed with thick wild woods, broken up by flower filled meadows, dark green marshland and ruddy bogs. It was so beautiful I forgot all about the pain in my bum.

"It reminds me of Cornwall," a blue winged girl the size of my hand said with a sigh as she landed on my shoulder, "I miss Cornwall."

"I've never been to Cornwall," I replied.

"More like Scotland," said Nettle, "but with more trees."

"I've never been to Scotland either."

"You could say…" Cornflower - the tiny blue girl – proclaimed, "it's the best bits of just about everywhere. Except, there's no beach," she added and flew off.

"There's no beach!" Nettle gasped, "I've never noticed that before! There's no beach. Why can't we have a beach? It's not fair, where's our beach?" Nettle very quickly got himself worked up into a prickly rage.

"Actually Nettle, I think it's beautiful, it's just perfect."

"Yes, well it was… until somebody mentioned beaches," he said sulkily.

"Who needs beaches when you've got all this? Is this really real? I mean how can this be here, and nobody notice? What about planes? Satellites? Can they see it from space? Is it magic?"

Nettle scratched his head, then stroked the needles on his arm and thought for a long time; then said slowly, "I don't do magic. I just plant nettles and watch them grow. Nobody notices nettles, not until they walk into them that is, and after that…well people avoid them. Humans rarely notice the nettles delicate flowers, or the caterpillars that depend on them. They miss it all in trying to avoid getting stung… maybe it works the same way for Avalon. Nobody sees it because nobody's looking."

"I'm not sure that makes any sense Nettle but you are the wisest nettle bush I've ever met."

"Sharp as a nettle me. Race you!" and with that he rolled himself up into a ball and threw himself down the hill, yipping, laughing and hollering, rolling faster and further away. I wasn't going to miss out on that kind of fun. I threw my arms up and ran down the hill after him. Halfway down or less, I'd tripped over something, and went sprawling. I turned over and there were Thorn's eyes, flashing white lightening down at me.

"Where do you think you're going?"

"I'm just following Nettle, Fiddle showed me the bridge…"

"Not today Bottle," he bent down and grabbed me by the foot and started dragging me back up the hill.

"Let me go!" I shouted. "It's not fair. You can't do this!" I wasn't going to get so close to a magical land and then not be allowed to see it. "Let me go!" I twisted round and dug my fingers into the earth but Thorn just kept going. We reached the standing stones all too quickly but at least it gave me something solid to grab hold onto, I wasn't giving up that easily.

"Let go or I'll cut off your fingers," Thorn growled.

"No! I want to go into Avalon! You can't stop me."

Thorn whistled and moments later the air was filled with a frantic buzzing, as a hundred tiny-winged creatures landed on top of me. Tiny pin sharp fingers gripped my shoulders, arms and fingers – and dug in; I let go with a yelp! And then, I was flying.

The winged Good Folk pulled on my hair, clothes and ears and in a second, I was going up, up, up and then dipping down, down, down. I was clearly too heavy for the aged tiny Good Folk. The huge gapping chasm appeared below me, I felt my stomach drop down into it, and my head spin as if I was already falling.

"The oldest of the Good Folk are the smallest and most mischievous, let's hope they don't weaken or decide to drop you," Thorn sniggered.

I shut my eyes and held my breath and started counting backwards from twenty, but I never got to ten - as the whirring of wings stopped and I really was falling.

Chapter 5

My scream was cut short by my sudden collision with the edge of the precipice.

"Oh look, you made it," Thorn laughed like a rattling shard of ice. He grabbed the back of my neck and carried me back through the farmhouse kitchen and into the lobby, where he set me back on my feet; "go through that door, they're waiting." He was pointing at the last door on the left, the one next to the kitchen door.

"Who's waiting? Who's in there?"

"Go up the stairs and then you'll find out."

"What if I don't want to?"

The door opened.

"But it wants you Bottle," Thorn put one foot on the wall opposite the door, twisted his body round in the narrow space and then put his other foot on the ceiling; and so stood upside down before me, his face next to mine. "Maybe it's hungry?" he whispered. "Maybe it has gifts, maybe it has gold and jewels…"

"I don't want gold and jewels."

"Of course you do, you're human. You kept the money we gave you didn't you? What do you call it, the change?"

"That's not fair!" I shouted, "I tried to give it back to Fiddle but he wouldn't take it!"

"Of course you did," he said mockingly.

"I did! Ask Fiddle."

"Why? We all know he's a liar. You can give me the change now, if you want to."

I dug into my pockets and held out a fist full of money to him. Thorn sniffed it and sat cross-legged on the ceiling. "No, you keep it…it smells of human. I couldn't touch it."

I was so angry, I had to get away from him before I did something I really would regret. So I stepped through the open door, and slammed it shut behind me.

As soon as the door closed I was in total darkness, I stepped forward and my ankles collided with something hard, it felt like a wooden step, followed by another… it was stairs, uneven, dirty wooden stairs. There was only one thing to do, and I did it, I started to climb. My anger had given me some courage and some energy, but both soon started to melt. The stairway smelt stale and mouldy, like clothes that have been left too long in a washing machine. The staircase was very steep and narrow, more like a ladder really and it had to be climbed like one. Have you ever climbed a dusty, stinky ladder in the dark? I can't recommend it.

"Can you get poisoned by dust?" I asked myself, and then all the other questions started echoing about me – but not in my voice, in harsh, high-pitched, mocking fairy voices: What if you slip? What if the next step collapses? What if you fall? How far will you fall? Will you break a leg or your neck? Would anybody care?

"Yeah, my dad would care," I insisted, "and Mum too." I took a breath and kept on climbing.

At first, the steps had been hard going because of the dark and the dirt, cobwebs and grime. But I didn't worry about getting dirty for long, after all you can only get so dirty. I'd been climbing for at least five minutes but there was still nothing but darkness above me. I looked down and couldn't even see my own feet. I could feel my legs beginning to wobble. I had no idea how far I'd climbed. I decided to count the steps. If nothing else it would give me something to focus on! I was going to count them aloud but thought better of it. Fifteen, twenty, twenty-five and still more, thirty five! Where was I climbing to? The farmhouse wasn't that tall! Fifty-five, it had to be some kind of fairy trick! Maybe, there were three hundred more steps to come, or maybe three thousand, or maybe they would never end, and I'd be climbing forever.

And then I decided something that changed everything: I would just keep climbing until I couldn't climb anymore. I wasn't going to panic, and I wasn't going to give up! I would just keep going. And the strange thing is, although nothing had changed, it felt like everything had changed. I was scared but I was going to keep on going, and that made all the difference. I have learnt since then that this is what people call courage, being scared but carrying on.

Three steps later, my forehead hit a solid surface. I still couldn't see anything, but by reaching out and feeling about, I found two doorknobs, one on either side of me. One was round and the other felt like an 'L' shaped handle; and where there's a door handle, there's usually a door – so which to choose?

To be honest, by then, I really didn't care. I just wanted to get off of those stairs and out of the dark, but an idea popped into my head. I knocked on both doors at the same time.

The 'L' shaped handle glowed red, and I almost had it in my hand when I heard, the light bubbling voice of a little girl coming from the door with a round knob; "Come in Bottle," it said – and I did.

The room was filled with the light of many lamps and too many candles to count. For a moment I was dazzled, and then the room darkened. All the candles had gone out, and the lamps dimmed. The room filled with smoke and felt very cold. I waved the smoke away and could see a huge brass bed, at the far end of the room, covered with cushions and blankets. Sitting in the bed was the oldest lady I'd ever seen.

"Hello Bottle," she said in a voice as dry as sand.

"Hello… sorry I thought I heard…" I looked around for the little girl I'd heard from outside the door. She was nowhere to be seen, and there was nowhere in the room she could hide, unless she was under the bed. I stepped towards the bed and the room filled with light again. The lamps became brighter, and the candles reignited, and then I could see there was a little girl sitting in the bed, not an old woman at all. My eyes must have been playing tricks on me. "Hello… what's your name?" I asked her, "hold on… shouldn't I know your name?"

"Would that be because of the Contract?" she smiled and instantly turned into a beautiful woman with long dark hair and black eyes. As she did so the lamps went out and only the candles burned. "I have many names, none of them are me, but all of them are mine."

I had no idea what that meant, "Do you do that often?"

"Do I do what, Bottle of the Contract?"

"Change, from one person to another."

"I do not change, I am always the same," she replied with a stretch.

"So…what do I call you?"

"What you will. It matters little, it changes me none," she smiled and was suddenly the old lady I'd seen when I'd walked in, and just as quickly the lamps went on and the candles went out and I was surrounded by smoke again.

"And there you go again…"

"I haven't gone anywhere dearie; does it bother you?"

"No…" I said honestly, "though I don't know why it doesn't… should it bother me?"

"No, of course not. Change is constant, change is life, you understand this truth," the beautiful lady answered.

"Not normally," I confessed, "but for some reason I do today."

"So, you have also changed. It is the way," the little girl smiled sweetly at me. "But for you we will slow the waters, tell me Bottle who would you rather talk to?" All three of her forms flashed in front of me, one after another.

"I really don't mind," I said.

"Choose. You have to learn to choose."

The faces of the girl, woman and old women flashed before me faster and faster.

"Old lady please," I shouted.

The lights dimmed and the old lady sat before me on the bed. "Well-chosen Bottle. I am often called the Crone for my role in the circle. Tell me why you chose this face?"

"I don't know. I had a Nanna. My Gran she was always very nice. She knew a lot of things, because she was old, and if I'm to understand anything about this place, I have to talk to someone who knows what's going on."

"A good answer," the Crone nodded and beckoned for me to sit next to her, "come sit by me young one," and her voice was so warm and calm that I did.

The Crone's skin was so white and thin I could almost see through it. She seemed to creak and crack as she moved. She reached out a chalky finger and took hold of my chin, her thin wiry hair had fallen across her face, but her eyes were so bright they shone like blue flashlights.

"You are a bottle full of fears Bottle," she said as she squeezed my face, "how did this happen?"

"I don't know what you mean."

"Yes, you do. You are too young to be so afraid, you quiver like a willow tree in the fall."

"I'm not afraid…" I began to protest but her paper dry fingers tightened on my face and her eyes glowed orange and red. I stared into their flickering orange flame and felt myself beginning to lighten and drift away, falling into sleep.

I opened my eyes and found I was home. I was in my kitchen, but I knew I wasn't. My body was sitting on Crone's bed but somehow part of both of us was standing together in my house, moving like shadows across the kitchen floor.

"Be still child and walk with your mind," I heard the Crone whisper from a long way off.

In my mind I took hold of her hand, and together we moved like a draft through the gap in the kitchen door. Up the stairs we went and into my room, floating across the floor, across my toys and all the clothes I should have picked up, "Children and Good Folk have much in common," the Crone giggled. I had a picture of Mum beside my bed. I could see a dim reflection of myself within it, sitting on the bed looking into the photo. Mum looked happy in it, happy and well, just the way I wanted to remember her.

"Where is she child?"

"I do wish you people would stop calling me child," I heard myself say, "my mum's in a hospital… but it's not really a hospital. You stay there when you're…" I bit my lip, "the doctor says, when she comes home it will mean she's ready…" I choked on the words.

"To die," the Crone said plainly.

I nodded and my Mums picture disappeared, and I was back in the Crone's bedroom, with her arm across my back holding me tightly, rocking back and forth, her dry bones creaking like an unoiled swing.

"Humans fear what they do not understand, so they try to explain it all away, and fear it even more. I know what it is to lose a loved one."

The shadows drifted out beyond us but this time to an age long ago. We were part of a crowd of people, watching dancers skip around a tree. The tree had been ripped out of the ground and then planted upside down with its roots sticking up in the air.

"Where are we?" I asked.

"Here. This is my memory."

A young couple broke through the dancers and stood directly under the tree, and the whole crowd cheered them. The girl's face was full of laughter, her hair full of flowers, and the young man, who held her hand was dressed in a gown of flowers and straw, his face painted green.

"Is this a wedding?" I asked.

"It is Beltane. A joining between the Fairy Kingdom we call Avalon and the world of men. Watch…"

The dancers faded away and when they came back their faces and clothes had changed, but still they danced, and then they faded and changed again. The dancers became children, boys in flat caps and girls in white pinafores, dancing to the sound of a great brass band,

as they circled a Maypole swathed in brightly coloured ribbons, and Union Jack flags. Again, the dances changed, and the boys became bearded men in white shirts and trousers, dancing in line, with bells tied to their ankles, waving wooden sticks to the sound of fiddles and rasping squeezeboxes. And then women re-joined the dance, wearing denim dungarees, and hats full of flowers – and the dancers changed again and again, but the dance remained.

"Why are you showing me this?" I asked.

"We need your help to prepare for this year's Beltane."

"I know, you need me to do the shopping."

The Crone shook from head to toe with a dry dusty hacking cough of a laugh. "No, we need you for so much more, we need you to bring us the Green Man."

"Okay, where is he?"

"No, you must find us a Green Man. He must be human. The farmer is dead, so we need someone to play his part. You must find us a new Green Man."

"How?"

She stroked my hair and pinched my cheek. "You are smart Bottle; you'll work it out."

"And what if I can't?"

"Then the last days of the Kingdom of Avalon are here. Without the Beltane dance and the Green Man, our dance will end," the Crone put her creaking fingers to my lips, "you will find him, or we will die. Sleep now. Sleep."

I felt my eyes shut and the world begin to drift away again but the problem the Crone had given me lodged in my head. I wanted to save Avalon, I would if I could but how? How could I find them a Green Man? I heard a crow call or was it a laugh echoing in the distance and then the world fell into silence.

Chapter 6

I woke up with a pain in my back. I was lying on the farmhouse's doorstep, and it was nearly dark. Dark, as in nighttime: I should have been at home.

I jumped up and ran down the drive like my pants were on fire. Dad was going to kill me. I ran until my sides ached and I felt sick. I was very late and bound to be in trouble.

I opened the front door, kicked off my shoes, and walked into the kitchen, there was no one there. "Dad!" I called out, but there was no answer. Where was he? I was overwhelmed with the worst thoughts – something had happened to Mum and… and then I heard the key in the door.

"Hello there, all right? Sorry I'm late, I've just been up to see Mum, you eaten?"

"No, how is she?"

"Tired, we'll both go up tomorrow. I just thought you could do with a break. Beans of toast do?"

I nodded and then as Dad moved past me to go to the kitchen I grabbed his hand and squeezed.

"Dad is Mum scared?"

Dad dropped down onto one knee and put his other hand on my shoulder, "no love, she's not, are you?"

"Sometimes… not as much as I was."

"It scares me too, but not as much as it did. Because I've got you and I know you're going to be okay. We both are. I know it's not been easy, but we'll be okay," he squeezed my hand and we walked into the kitchen together.

Later that night as I was getting undressed, something fell out of my pocket and onto the floor. It was a roll of twenty-pound notes. Six hundred pounds wrapped around another shopping list, twice as long as the first one, "Do they expect me to find a Green Man," I said, "or buy one? Where would I buy a Green Man?" And then I remembered the old man in the superstore, throwing around the apples… had I already seen the Green Man?

Here's another question for you; where do milkmen get their milk? And don't say cows. Here's how they used to do it; Dad would drive out to the dairy depot at about four o'clock in the morning. He'd figure out how many crates of milk we needed – as well as loaves of bread, eggs, yoghurt and cream – then load everything onto the float, and then the day's work would really begin.

At the weekends I'd meet Dad as he came back into the estate. I'd have a flask of coffee made up and some sandwiches and then we'd get stuck into the round. On the day in question, I decided to get up with Dad, and help him at the depot, that way I figured he wouldn't mind too much if I finished early again. I'd go down to the superstore, get the Good Folk's shopping, have a quick look around Avalon, and still be back home again in time to meet up with Dad and go visit Mum at the hospice – there's a poem by Robert Burns says; "The best laid schemes o' mice an' men / Gang aft a-gley." – gang aft a-gley is right.

We were loading up the milk-float when this old fella with a thick grey beard and an old flat cap came over to us. He nodded at me and then called Dad to one side. I jumped into the cab and started thumbing through the delivery ledger, but all the time I was listening to them talk about the loss of business, the shrinking rounds, and supermarket prices and something called 'franchises' – I didn't know what that was, but by the look on Dad's face when he climbed into the cab, I knew it wasn't good news; "what's wrong?"

"That's Ol'Bob, he's been doing this for twenty years. He says he's lost four accounts in the last week. Reckons it's due to the new superstore. Let's hope we don't have the same trouble."

That morning, I found three notes: all from regular customers cancelling their accounts.

"It's that superstore," Dad kept saying, "they're under cutting the dairy."

I'd better explain that; the problem was the superstore was so close to the estate that people living there could get their milk from it at a cheaper rate than the dairy could sell it. And it was cheaper, because the store owners had so many stores, they bought milk in bulk and so could sell it cheaper than the dairy that supplied the milk. And that's why you've probably never seen a milk-float.

By the time we reached the edge of the estate Dad was in a silent fume. And when we saw the roadside billboard announcing, 'new local SUPERSTORE only '500 yards away,' I thought he was going to explode.

"Do you mind if I jump out here Dad?"

"Places to be?"

"Kind of... meet up back home later and then go see Mum, okay."

Dad just nodded and drove on.

Perhaps it would have been kind to stay with Dad for the whole round, but I didn't really understand what he was going through, and I had my own problems to solve – how not to get eaten, how to find the Green Man and how to fit eighty Easter eggs into a shopping trolley.

Yes, eighty Easter eggs, that was the sum total of the Good Folk's shopping list. One trolley was not going to be enough. I grabbed another and pressed them together side by side, and the first face I saw as I entered the store was? The security guard, and of course he wasn't there to offer any help. No none of that. He decided to follow me around the store, it was as if he'd never seen a child shopping alone with two trolleys before.

Getting eighty Easter eggs into two trolleys is not easy. I started throwing an assortment of eggs from different shelves into the trolley but that was going to fill them up too quickly, so I started again and stuck to a box with a fluffy yellow chick on the front. This meant I could stack them up more easily, but it wasn't much better, because as soon as I moved, they toppled over. Having two trolleys didn't exactly help. I was bumping into the racks, bumping into people and sending Easter eggs tumbling all over the place. My hovering security guard wasn't amused; "What ya think ya doin'?!"

I was about to explain when, a woman with angry hair and the same complexion as a London bus screamed, "you've taken all the eggs! You can't have all the eggs! I want some eggs."

"There are other eggs," I replied, and there were lots of other Easter eggs.

"I don't want those, I want those Easter eggs, I like those Easter eggs! You can't do that! Get the manager!" she shouted getting redder and redder in the face as she did so, "get the manager."

The security guard gave me this sour smile and said, "gladly," and squawked into his walky-talky thing, moments later a lady in a tight blue suit turned up.

"Hello, I'm Tricia the store manager, how can I help you today?" she said with a grin as thin as a razor.

"I want those Easter eggs," the lady with angry hair shouted, "that brat's taken all the Easter eggs!"

"There are other Easter eggs available," Tricia pointed out.

"I want those Easter eggs!" the woman shouted, "I came in here for those Easter eggs and I'm not leaving until I've got some. He's not allowed to take all the eggs. It shouldn't be allowed!" she finished with a wheeze, leaning against a rack for support.

"This one was in here yesterday buying Easter eggs!" the security guard blurted out pointing at me accusingly.

"I see," Tricia said patiently, "now then, do you really need all those Easter eggs?"

I nodded, "I do."

"So many?"

I showed her the shopping list which very clearly said eighty Easter eggs.

"I see," she sniffed, "and do you have the money to pay for all of this?"

Yet another adult, thinking I was playing shop; until I showed her the money.

"I see…well in that case," she said, "would you mind swapping out some of these so this lady, can have some of those particular eggs?"

As I looked at the unsteady tower in my trolley, an idea occurred to me, "no I don't mind at all, as long as he helps me take them to the checkout."

"Oh, I'm sure we can do that. Well, there go then, that's sorted."

The red-faced woman deflated, as the security guard's face ignited – but he helped me just the same, seething every step of the way; it was the same lady on the checkout as had been there the day before.

"See to this, will you Edith," the guard hissed, throwing an armful of the boxes onto the conveyor belt, and storming away.

"Hello, you, shopping again, more party food?" Edith chuckled, "you have a lot of parties, it must be fun at your house."

"Yes, I think it must be."

"Think? Don't you go to the parties?" she asked with a concerned look.

"Well…yes. But it's mostly for adults."

She looked even more worried at this.

"That is," she was making me nervous, "I go to bed and then they have the party," I mumbled, "but they do give me some cake…and I don't really like chocolate."

"Are you all right dear?" Edith asked very gently, "are you in trouble? Is everything alright?"

"Yes, really everything's fine really," I could see she didn't believe me. When we'd finally got the Easter eggs back into the trolley – Edith did a much better job of it - and I went to hand over the roll of money, she took hold of my hand.

"If you need someone to talk to dear, I'm always here or I could give you my phone number."

All I could do was smile and thank her. I pushed my trolleys away as quickly as I could. I looked over my shoulder and saw Edith talking with the fuming security guard. I decided right then and there, even if the Good Folk threatened to chew off my toes, I wasn't going back to that store ever again.

Chapter 7

Loading eighty Easter eggs into the taxi wasn't easy but thankfully the same baldheaded taxi driver turned up and was very helpful, and we were soon off down Lone Farm Road. But as soon as we got out of the taxi, I knew we were in for trouble: because a nettle bush nodded at me.

We were unloading the bags, when we heard a cuckoo, the driver stopped what he was doing, and looked up into the trees, "did you hear that?" he said, "first cuckoo of spring. I can't remember the last time I heard a cuckoo, I must have been a boy…"

The cuckoo sounded again, and this time, very close behind us. The driver spun around, looking into the tops of the trees as he did so; and then the cuckoo sounded behind us, and he spun back. I saw the nettle bush move, and something that looked like a twisted walking stick dropped at the driver's feet. The cuckoo called again and once again the driver turned; caught himself in the stick and fell face first into the nettle bush.

"Ow! Ow! Ow!" he yelped, jumping to his feet, rubbing franticly at his welt covered face - until he heard a high-pitched giggle. "So, you think that's funny do you?!" he shouted looking at me, "do you think that's funny?"

The giggle came again but this time he saw it wasn't me.

"Who's there? Who is it?!"

"Bald as a boiled egg," the giggling voice snorted.

"Who said that?" the taxi driver shouted, but no answer came, so he stamped and shouted some more. "Who is it? Who's there? Come on show yourself! Right then!" he declared pointing at me, "you're behind this! Don't you think I don't know it!"

"Baldy bum," giggled the nettle bush. Without thinking the furious man plunged his hands into the bush to pull out the naughty child he thought was there, and instantly regretted it.

"Ahhh!" he screamed, "right you! Don't you ever call this taxi line again, you hear me, you're banned! You hear me banned!" and with that he threw the rest of the Easter eggs onto the ground, jumped into his car and sped off, shouting all the way down the bumpy road.

Nettle heaved and shook with laughter, "Did you see that? I haven't had so much fun in ages!"

"That was really mean," I insisted, although I could feel a smile rising within me.

Fiddle kicked himself upright with a gasp, "that was great."

"That was really mean," I repeated, doing my best to sound serious.

"I know," Fiddle wheezed, "but wasn't it brilliant! Oh there was a time when we could put the wind up a whole village, a whole village! We'd have them running off down the road screaming for their mothers... good times, good times."

The earth beneath my feet rumbled as Hill stepped out of the trees chuckling like a baby, "do it again, do it again.'

Elf arrows," Nettle said with a wink, "I remember the first time I heard humans talking about elf arrows, I was a sapling back then," he looked at me, knowing full well I had no idea what he was talking about, "you see Bottle, humans once believed we could make them ill with our invisible Elf arrows. Utter nonsense of course but we played along, they blamed us for everything, from the boils on their bums to the plague, good days, Bottle, good days."

"Do it again!" Hill chuckled until the leaves on the trees quivered, "Do it again!"

"Hill," Fiddle snapped, "the man has gone, the car has gone. Can you see that? We can't do it again because...?"

"Gone," Hill rumbled sadly, "Green Man gone, car gone. Avalon gone."

"Not before we get the shopping in," Fiddle sighed, "come on then you lot! Let's get this lot in before more stinky humans turn up and build something."

A swarm of the smaller winged creatures flew out from their hiding places and began pilling the Easter eggs high upon Hill's broad back, and off they went, back to the house.

"Why don't you like humans?" I had to ask.

"You're too busy naming things or knocking things down and building them up again – look there's a wall! Let's knock it down and build another wall, and call it wall, just like the last wall," Fiddle stamped.

"What's wrong with naming things?"

Fiddle scratched his wooden head, "because you think if you name something, you own it. And you don't," he stamped away then turned back and wagged his knitting needle finger at me, "and then you change the meaning and the words, and it's very annoying!"

"Easter eggs, for example," a very proper voice asserted from behind me. It was a very upright and tidy looking hare. It was sitting on its back legs, black tipped ears pointing up to the sky, "do you know why you call them Easter eggs?" it asked, and then set off at a dash to catch up with the others.

"Well…" I realised I had no idea. "no, I don't know."

The hare being a hare had already overtaken the other Good Folk and then with a kick of dust, it turned on its heels and ran back to me and sat on its hind legs as it wagged its paw at me, "Easter used to be Eoster. You've changed names and lost the meaning," and with that he flicked his ears back and sped off.

"I have no idea what you're talking about."

"Which proves my point," Fiddle yelled as he pushed open the farmhouse door, "it's very annoying!"

"I think people just like eating chocolate eggs," I stated a little weakly.

"Eat them!" Fiddle cried, "you eat them. We don't eat them! And you won't either. You don't even touch them! Remember what I said? That which is Avalon's stays in Avalon."

"You're not going to eat them, so why do you want so many? Why did I just buy eighty Easter eggs?"

"Beltane offerings obviously. We need the May Queen and the Green Man to get together, what else would you have us offer? And you're meant to be out there looking for him aren't you? Beltane isn't far off. You have been looking haven't you?"

"That's not easy to do when someone keeps sending you to do their shopping." I thought this was a very clever thing to say, but the Good Folk didn't hear me. They'd already disappeared into the house. I followed them but the door was slammed shut in my face.

I stepped back and waited but this time the door didn't open. I stood there feeling hurt and dejected and then I decided I wasn't going to let them get away with it. Good Folk or not, bad manners were still bad manners, and I wasn't going to let them push me around. I pushed the door open and stamped into the kitchen.

The fire was lit and the cauldron bubbling, around it sat many bedraggled looking Good Folk, all staring gloomily into the flames.

"What's wrong?" I asked, immediately forgetting how angry I was with them.

"It's the bridge," said a long slender creature called Ivy who sat sprawling across the floor, "it's fallen into the ravine and now we cannot reach Avalon."

"Well, I'm not surprised, it didn't look very safe to me. What's the problem? Can't you just fly or magic yourself across?" I asked.

"Wish that we could," Nettle sighed, "but we don't all have that ability, some of the older ones can fly but this is where the cauldron is, so it's a problem."

I couldn't see what the problem was, "Can't you just fly the cauldron across then? It can't be that heavy."

"An oak couldn't be thicker,' Fiddle snapped, "keep your daft notions to yourself human."

"The cauldron is the hearth and the gate," Ivy explained, wrapping a delicate arm around my shoulders, "if we move the cauldron into Avalon, our boundary will shrink to fit around it and many homes will be lost, and with them many lives. The great living oaks, the humming rocks, the bog of bliss where the frogs of forgetfulness live, all these would be lost."

"We have to repair the bridge," Owl stated, swiveling its head around, "but we don't know how."

"Building stuff, isn't really our thing," said Nettle, shuffling his leaves self-consciously.

"Our thing?" sniped Fiddle, "all you're good for is hedgerow tea."

"That's rich coming from an overgrown spoon!" Nettle retorted.

"You weed!" Fiddle shouted back.

"Firewood!" Nettle sneered, rustling his leaves angrily.

"Enough!" a dry voice rasped, and there standing beside me was the Crone. She coughed, took my hand and changed into the little girl and said, "the Green Man would know what to do," but then turned into the beautiful woman and seemed to fill with determination, "now listen my children, we have a problem that must be solved if we are to survive, but do not fret, for we have with us a child of man," she squeezed my hand, "and man loves to build. Isn't that so Bottle?"

"I've never built anything," I blurted.

She smiled kindly, "your tribe were not blessed with many gifts. But you built your own. You've built houses and dwellings all over this world, and built machines to take you to and fro, across seas and to other worlds; it is in your blood to create. It is your gift and your curse. Surely you can think of a means to take us across the divide," she smiled and changed back into the Crone.

All eyes fell on me, expectant and hopeful, and completely convinced of my ability as a human child to build a bridge.

"I wouldn't know where to start," I said.

"I would suggest starting on this side, as it's closer," Fiddle suggested most unhelpfully.

What else could I do? "Okay then... let's have a look at the problem."

A huge crowd of creatures had gathered on the stranded side, some were flying above the ravine but many of the larger and stranger folk sat in the mist that flowed through the ring of stones, dejected and weeping. Sitting on the edge of the cliff with his feet dangling over the edge was Thorn, his diamond eyes sparkling as he watched me, "Greetings Bottle," he called across, "any bright ideas?"

"Couldn't we cut down a tree?" said I, thinking aloud.

A gasp of horror came from the crowd.

"That'll be a no then," Thorn sneered.

"Can you get over here?" I asked, "couldn't they carry you over?"

Thorn picked up a stone and threw it straight at my head, but just as it reached the middle of the divide it dropped straight down out of sight. The Good Folk groaned ominously.

"We gain our strength from the hearth Bottle," Thorn shouted across, "the old ones may not last much longer without access to the cauldron."

"What will happen to them?"

"You see those standing stones," the Crone answered turning into the beautiful lady as she pointed across the ravine, "the last time the bridge collapsed they were Hill's brothers."

"So this has happened before. What did you do?"

"The farmer built a bridge. Or was it the farmer's grandfather? I can't recall. All your faces look the same, it's very confusing."

"But I don't know what to do" and how could I? "This is a job for engineers and grown-ups."

"But we don't have any of those here Bottle, so you'll have to do. If only we had the May Queen and her Green Man residing yonder, the magic would be strong enough to restore the bridge, but alas," the Crone added quietly putting one bony hand on my shoulder, "have you had any luck with finding our Green Man yet?"

"No, no yet," I snapped, "I haven't had a chance. I've been too busy doing your shopping. And I can't build bridges!"

"Very well then," Fiddle creaked, "sit there and do nothing, sit there and watch us turn to stone."

"It's true," the Crone shrugged, "without the connection to the hearth, they will be gone by dawn."

Chapter 8

I shut my eyes and thought hard. What else could we use as a bridge if we couldn't cut down trees? After all a bridge is just something you lay across a gap, how difficult could it be? What's good to build with? I jumped up, shouting, "what's in the barn?" and then ran off to find out.

The biggest thickest cobweb I'd ever seen filled the barn from one corner to the next. It was so thick I could barely see the abandoned old farming equipment that was piled up to its roof.

"Can you clear the cobwebs away? I need to see what we've got…" I didn't need to explain.

There was a whirr of wings and giggles galore as a buzzing swarm of tiny Good Folk rushed into the barn and started gathering up bundles of cobwebs. Clouds of dust and muck filled the air, hiding everything from view, but as it began to settle, I could see the barn was very old but solidly built. It had huge wooden beams, some bent like the ribs of a huge whale, others that stretched from one end of the barn to the other. Some were blackened in a few places, where the roof tiles had given way, but the longest of the wooden beams looked as solid as the day they were cut.

"I think," I said, "we can do it. We're going to take down the barn."

I drew a plan in the dust, and pointed out what I wanted the Good Folk to do. Fiddle then pointed where I pointed, and Nettle pointed where he pointed, and soon everybody was pointing, and nobody knew what to do. But eventually I managed to get my plans across to the Good Folk and gave them all a job to do; not that the Good Folk are any good at following even the simplest instructions. As soon as the roof tiles were piled up, they were knocked over and had to be piled up again. The old farm equipment was pushed to one side of the barn; then immediately pushed to the other side, and then pushed to the back wall, where it was stacked into a tower that swayed so alarmingly even the Good Folk got nervous, and so it was taken down, restacked outside the barn, and thanks to a bumbling Hill, knocked into the ravine. The truth is, it was chaos, dirty, dusty chaos. Add to that the quarrels with the representatives of the pigeons and spiders we were making homeless, and it all took much longer than it needed to, but eventually the biggest wooden beams were lowered to the floor.

"Can you carry these to the edge and then lay them across the gap?" I asked Hill, who certainly looked strong enough for the task. Hill scratched his enormous flat head.

"I'm not sure that's a good idea," Fiddle whispered, "one task at a time is best with Hill. He's only a baby."

"Pretty big baby," I observed.

"His mother was a mountain. And he's still a baby, no matter his size," Fiddle insisted.

"All he has to do is lay it across the gap."

"And what if he drops it? What if he doesn't let go?"

I watched as Hill ate three roof tiles one after the other as if they were candy. Perhaps Fiddle had a point, "what we really need is a crane," I observed.

"We haven't had cranes in Albion for years, you lot killed them off," Fiddle sneered.

"A crane Fiddle not a Crane. It's a machine not a bird! It lifts heavy things."

"Once again, a name of a thing that isn't the thing! You humans, why do you keep changing the words!" Fiddle ranted, "its so annoying, when is a Crane not a crane? When it's a crane of course. I think I'm going to rub myself together until I burst into flame, it would be easier!"

"What if I turned you into a golf club?" I whispered through gritted teeth, "look, we've got the beam down. All we need to do is dig a trench. A slot in the ground on both sides for the beam to slot into, and then we drop the beam into the slots, surely, we can manage that."

"I see," said Fiddle unconvincingly, "we could really do with Dig, Dug and Ditch, but alas we lost them years ago. They were eaten by a metal dragon somewhere near Dulwich…"

"A dragon!" I exclaimed.

"Yes, one of man's metal creations. But don't let yourself be distracted Bottle, you need to focus on the job at hand. Which…." He seemed to be having problems remembering the job at hand, and then, with a firm stamp proclaimed, "Digging! Digging is something we can do. Mole and Badger!"

Two mud covered creatures with large square shaped paws pushed their way through the crowd and bowed.

"Listen carefully you two," Fiddle snapped, "we need you to open up a surface burrow. This wide and this deep and that way," he signaled with the sharp angles of his flapping arms, "get to it!" Fiddle then shouted the same instructions across the divide to Thorn, who took charge of business on that side. Soon there was a flurry of digging and flying mud on both sides of the ravine and in moments the slots we needed were done.

"We know how to dig," Fiddle smiled proudly, "we are the people of the hollow hills."

"Well done," I said but rather flatly. Seeing the slots for the beam, just made the placing of the beam seem more impossible. The collective strength of the Good Folk had struggled to lower it to the ground. If Hill couldn't be trusted to lift it, I didn't know what to do, "and now we're stuck."

Nettle stepped up to the beam, gave it a lick and then rolled the flavour around his mouth, "maybe not… in my opinion," he said, crossing his arms, "we are going to need the Haggis."

The gathered Good Folk instantly broke into a spontaneous round of applause and Nettle took a bow; they clearly all agreed.

"Must we wake him?" the Crone asked reluctantly.

"I regret we must my lady, only the Haggis has the strength and skill we need," Nettle stated, "I think it's what he would want."

The Crone nodded sadly, and then pointed to Fiddle, who bowed in response, clicked his elbows together three times, and began to mark out a beat with his knees. The gathered host began to hum. Now the tune they made is difficult to describe, but it was high and sweet and sounded like wind whistling through tuned reeds, and then it became a mixture of sweetness and the cry of an unhappy cat and then it became ten, twenty, thirty unhappy cats, and just when I thought my ears would burst – in came four Good Folk, who looked like charcoal sticks with red hats solemnly carrying a small wooden box. They bowed to the Crone who was sitting on Hill's back and placed the box at her feet. The Crone transformed into the young girl and spoke clearly to the crowd in a beautiful sing song voice.

"He is the last of his kind and precious to us. He rests to conserve his life and to hide from his loneliness. Pray silence for the Haggis."

"Isn't that some kind of food?" I asked Fiddle. I was instantly shushed.

The young girl knocked gently three times on top of the box. "Dear one. We have need of your ancient craft, come and play, and sport with us, as once you did in the days of old. Rise once again and let us see the beauty of your face. We need you my brother, come save Avalon, for you are the glory of our race."

The lid of the box opened and fell to the floor. In it sat a drab brown round creature with a short stubby nose and pin prick black eyes that twinkled like far away stars. It nodded to the gathered crowd and then to the little girl who changed into the woman as she bowed in return. It then looked around, saw me and – although it had no mouth I could see – smiled; and then slowly climbed out of the box.

Fiddle stepped forward, bowed to the Haggis and then pointed to the plan on the floor, to the beam and then to the slots made in the earth. The tiny brown creature nodded, licked his stubby fingers, wriggled his nose and waddled off down to the far end of the beam. The Good Folk started their strange ugly song; it was not dissimilar to the sound a set of wet bagpipes might make.

The Haggis reached the far end of the beam and drummed his plump belly with his fingers – all fell silent. The Haggis bent its incredibly small legs, dropping its belly to the floor, and grabbed hold of the beam – all gasped. The Haggis' eyes twinkled, as with a hop it lifted the end of the beam high above its head so that it stood directly under it. For a moment it looked as if the weight would squash the Haggis flat, and then, bam! The Haggis jumped and threw the end of the beam upright into the air! Quick as a wink, the Haggis ran to the other end of the beam and lifted the whole thing off the ground.

The song of the Good Folk grew deafeningly loud, and cheers and bellows of encouragement rang out, as the mighty Haggis carried the swaying beam away from the dismantled barn and down along the narrow cliff edge. It then hopped from one foot to another as it turned to face the freshly dug slots. We all fell silent.

The Haggis hopped forward, paused, swayed and then threw the beam high into the air. I watched it spin upwards, turning over and over, top to tail, as it flew across the ravine; and then, CRASH! It fell perfectly into the dug slots.

We all cheered and clapped. The Good Folk who had been trapped on the other side ran across the beam as if it was as wide as a road and danced into the arms of their friends. They were wild with joy and the celebrations could have gone on for days if the Crone hadn't suddenly thrown her head back and howled like a wounded dog. The Good Folk fell silent, and all eyes turned back to the Haggis.

The Haggis bowed to his friends, and then its round brown shoulders slumped as he slowly made his way back to the barn. The sad humming song began again, more quietly now for many of the singers were crying. A slight prickly looking creature stepped into the Haggis' path and handed him a thistle; the Haggis took it and grasped it to its little round belly. He sighed deeply and ran the rest of the way to his box. On reaching it, he bowed to the Crone, climbed back in, and laid down, with the thistle held tightly under his nose. The Crone replaced the lid and stroked it silently before the thin charcoal figures solemnly carried it past a long line of weeping Good Folk, taking the Haggis back to its final resting place.

"He was the best of us," Nettle sighed, shaking tears from his leaves.

Chapter 9

Once the first beam was in place the rest was easy, now there were more than enough hands willing to get the work done. The Good Folk wouldn't even consider using nails to make the job easier. Fiddle said they couldn't bear to touch iron, so the crossbeams were tied down using rope the Good Folk had spun from grass and reeds, and it seemed to do the job well enough. To test the bridge, they sent Hill out to stand in the middle of it.

"But what if he falls?" I asked.

"Well as long as he doesn't break the bridge I wouldn't worry," Fiddle said with a shrug.

"But you said he was only a baby, 'what if he falls' you said."

"Did I?" Fiddle said with some surprise, "oh you don't want to be listening to me. I'm sure he'd find his way back up. Eventually."

Now Hill wasn't too keen on the idea either, but they managed to push him to the edge of the bridge and then with Thorn using Fiddle as a poker – which Fiddle didn't like – and a bunch of Good Folk called the Daffs tempting Hill across with roof tiles, Hill made his way out onto the bridge's centre. It creaked and it groaned, it even bowed a little, but thankfully and wonderfully it held.

"From this time on, "the Crone declared, " this bridge is known as Bottle's Bridge."

"Thank you, that's very kind of you but do you think perhaps, that Haggis Bridge would be better?"

The Crone scratched the hairs on her chin and looked at me thoughtfully, "it is a noble thought Bottle, but Haggis Bridge doesn't sound as good as Bottle Bridge."

"What about 'The Haggis Hop'?" I suggested.

The Crone smiled and nodded. "From this day on, this bridge is called Haggis Hop."

The Good Folk cheered.

I was given the privilege of being the first to officially cross over Haggis Hop – of course as soon as my foot touched Avalon, a huge crowd of cheering Good Folk sped across, nearly flattening me in the rush. But I got up and brushed myself down – there really was no point in making a fuss, the Good Folk were determined to have a good time.

A large fire was built within the crescent of the standing stones and then food was brought across from the house and a party was soon underway.

No-one knows how to throw a party like the Good Folk. The last one you go to is always as good as the first and the first is better than any other party you've ever been to. There's lots of music and dancing, and then there are very funny speeches and because the Good Folk love playing tricks on each other there's always lots of outrageous things happening.

For example, Nettle loved to sneak behind people and try to sting their bottoms and then hide, so that someone else got the blame, and what's even stranger is that everybody thought this was hilarious – even those who had been stung!

Hill loved dancing, and danced so fast and hard, the ground shook with his bouncing. Everybody's drink got spilt, but nobody minded, and everybody laughed – or jumped up to cheer him on; only to sit back down again onto Nettle – and then scream with laughter.

The Crone sang a song about a giant called the Apple Man which had its own special dance which involved people dancing around in a circle whilst carrying wooden buckets full of water. The circles broke into pairs, who spun around and around each other until they couldn't stand up. The first person to fall over had his or her head ducked into a bucket of water. It looked like a lot of fun, but I gave it a miss.

Thorn told stories that he said were, "the real and original stories of Lore." One was about a very unpleasant princess, who was tricked into kissing a 'frog of forgetfulness,' which the Good Folk thought was very funny. Another was about a very brave troll who protected his bridge from three very rude goats and ended up having a lovely stew. Thorn told that one twice.

As well as all the dancing and joking, there were all sorts of 'Elf Sports;' I shall give you a couple of the worst examples.

The most popular was Dilly Dashing. This involves running blindfolded through standing stones, not around but through them. Let me explain; despite what you and I may see, standing stones are actually very indecisive things, and only stand still because they can't decide what to do next. The Good Folk are able to run through a 'doubting stone', but not through a 'certain stone' and it seems that stones change quickly from one to the other. The aim of the game is to run through a ring of stones as quickly as you can, pausing only for the stones to change their minds. The winner is the quickest one around the circle. The loser is knocked out of the game – literally – by running into a 'certain' stone. The blindfold is to hide the colour of the stone, as their colour makes the game too easy. I was told Hill isn't allowed to play this game as the stones were once his brothers, however I was also told he once played the game somewhere in Wiltshire, and got it so horribly wrong he broke the best stone circle the Good Folk ever had; the remains of which can be seen in Wiltshire to this day. You'll have to decide which story you believe for yourself.

Another game, which is not to be tried at home, is called 'Winking'. It involves two opponents facing each other winking very quickly at each other. The rules are very simple. You are not allowed to poke a winking eye. If you poke an unwinking eye you get one point, if you poke a winked eye you lose a point, the first person to twenty winks wins. It is very funny to watch but horrible to play, don't try it! Your eyes are not Good Folk eyes!

I was having a wonderful time watching everybody singing, dancing, Winking and Dilly Dashing, until Thorn in his grey green gown tapped me on the shoulder.

"Hungry Bottle?" he said offering me an apple.

"Yes actually, thanks." I nearly took it, but remembered what Fiddle had warned me, "then again maybe not."

A thin wicked smile crept over Thorn's pale face, "come on Bottle. You must be hungry. After all it's getting late," he grinned.

He was right. It was late, in fact it was nearly dark! I'd done it again. Dad had wanted us to visit Mum together, and I'd spent the best part of the day at Lone Farm. I really was for it this time. I ran across Haggis Hop and into the farmhouse with Thorn's nasty dry laugh ringing in my ears.

I ran as fast as I could, but the sky grew darker with every stride and before I reached the estate the streetlights were on. I until my sides ached and my head span, and when I reached my house, I was gasping and ready to puke.

Chapter 10

Dad was sitting at the kitchen table. He looked at me and my heart cracked. I could tell he'd been crying. I stood there waiting for him to shout at me, but he didn't, he just sat there saying nothing.

Now my heart was racing, "is Mum …?" I couldn't say the word.

"No son, no… your Mum's… "and then he couldn't find the words, "I don't think it's going to be long," he wiped his nose on his sleeve and sniffed, "she was asleep. She didn't know you weren't there… and I'm glad you weren't, but I think it's important you see her… before it's too late."

"I know. I want to, I intended to, I really did. I just lost track of time."

Dad sat back in his chair and looked at me with a frown, "where you been?"

"Playing."

"Who with?"

"No one really," I hated lying but what was I going to tell him?

"You're filthy, been making dens?"

"Bridges."

"Fantastic. Over in the woods?"

I nodded; it wasn't much of a lie as Lone Farm wasn't far from the woods.

"You've not eaten then? Cause we got nothing in," he asked with a yawn.

I shrugged and wiped my eyes "I am sorry Dad."

"Don't be, we'll go see your Mum early tomorrow straight after work," he stood up and stretched his back and then went to the sink and splashed cold water on his face, "well, early start or not, I'm not going to sleep much tonight, you tired?" I shook my head, "come on then scruff, let's get some food," he picked up his coat from the back of the chair and headed for the door, I ran after him.

Our car was called Gertrude – it was bright orange with orange hubcaps and Dad said it was the worst car in the world. Gertrude's heating didn't work, and the windscreen wipers only had one speed which was very fast and noisy. She never started first try, usually the third, sometimes the fifth and if she didn't start on the sixth try, she wasn't going to start at all – or at least not until Dad had opened the bonnet and cleaned the points – that's something old cars had, new cars have computers, and you can't clean them with an oily rag and a bit of spit. Gertrude was a terrible car, but I loved her. I loved the big comfy seats and the way she rattled and spluttered. I knew every bash and dent and tear in the upholstery.

She started second time and her engine sounded healthy and happy to be alive. I pulled one of the blankets we kept in the backseat over my lap and snuggled back into the big passenger seat and lost myself in the rattling din. I could smell Mum in that seat, I could smell her perfume and hear her laugh in between the metal creeks and groans. I hadn't felt tired when we left but it had been a wild working day and I must have drifted off because the next thing I knew Dad was poking my ribs and opening his door.

"Come on then you, I thought you weren't tired. Do you want to wait in the car?" he asked as he climbed out.

"No Dad," I said, as his door closed. I jumped out, slammed my door and there we were at the superstore.

Dread is a very strange feeling; you'll know if you've had it. It's cold on the outside and hot on the inside and makes everything seem horribly twisted and threatening. And from the moment Dad walked from the car to collect the trolley to the moment he walked through the doors, that is all I felt – and as soon as I saw that security guard it got worse.

I stuck as close to Dad as I could. I stared at the ground, but I knew the security guard had seen me because he followed us through fruit and veg, and past the bakery, and stood at the end of every aisle watching us suspiciously. He watched Dad get cornflakes, and he watched us load baked beans and tinned spaghetti into the trolley. He never took his horrible beady eyes off us.

"I think we're being followed," Dad whispered.

"Are we?" I said, trying to sound surprised.

"Yeah, it's that security guard. Do you know why?" I shook my head. "It's because you're so dirty, he thinks we're up to no good." Dad smiled and winked; he was enjoying it!

We moved round the end of the tinned produce aisle and found ourselves in the sweet and biscuit aisle, and who was loading Jammie Dodgers onto the shelves? Of course, it had to be Edith from the tills.

"Hello," she said.

"Hello. Alright?" Dad replied, with a broad grin, 'how you doing?'

"Fine thanks. No Easter eggs today then?" she said, and it sounded more like a statement than a question.

"No thank you; can't stand the things. Hot cross buns might be an idea though. Take care, see you later."

Edith's face dropped, and thankfully, we moved on quickly.

"Is she one of mine?" Dad asked me in a whisper.

"No Dad, I don't think so."

"I wasn't sure. You don't want an Easter egg do you? You're Mum usually deals with that sort of thing, do you want one?"

"No you're all right. I've gone right off them." I knew what had just happened. Luckily Dad thought Edith might have been one of his customers, and that was why she was saying hello, a lot of his customers did that, and he almost never recognised them. He said people looked different in their pajamas. I looked over my shoulder. Edith and the security guard were talking. I decided it was time to get out of there.

"Have we finished yet, I'm really tired," I said adding an extra loud yawn for effect.

Dad looked at the trolley and then at me.

"Yeah, I'm not sure why we came in here really. I fancy chips. Come on then," we took the trolley to a till being operated by a young woman with curly red hair and bright blue eye makeup, who didn't look at us once, even when she said; "Twenty-two pounds, ten pence please."

Dad patted down his coat, and turned bright red, "I seem to have forgotten my wallet. Can we put it aside or owe maybe you?"

"We don't do credit. I'll have to call the manager," the girl said with a snotty look and pushed a button that buzzed and lit up her till sign. The security guard started towards us.

I plunged my hand into my pocket and dropped to my knees, "hang on Dad, this fell out of your pocket," I said as I stood up, and offered him a twenty-pound note; twenty-pounds of the Good Folk's money.

Dad looked at me with a mixture of relief and bewilderment. He took the money and paid the girl. We couldn't get out of there fast enough. We loaded up Gertrude and jumped in. I really thought I'd gotten away with it.

Dad put the keys in the ignition and then turned to me. "Where'd you get that money Kay?"

"It fell out of your pocket."

"No it didn't. Don't lie to me," his eyes glared straight into mine, "where did you get it?" His face had that serious 'you are in trouble' look.

"I found it."

"Where?"

"In the woods."

"Where in the woods?" he asked tapping the dashboard with one hand; a signal that Dad was really getting annoyed.

I decided being near the truth was going to be better than making up another complete lie, "I got it from Lone Farm. I went to the farm, I just needed to see it. But when I got there, there were people there moving stuff out and they saw me. I said that we'd found the farmer and that you'd called the police, and they gave me the money," I shut my mouth, amazed and ashamed at my own capacity to lie.

Dad rubbed his head and lent on the steering wheel. "You know better than to talk to strangers Kay. And you never ever take money from them, never! You never keep a secret from me, especially if a stranger says you must! You know that."

"Yeah, I know."

"How much did they give you?"

"That was it, twenty-pounds," more lies, a huge lie, I couldn't look Dad in the eye; I felt terrible. But I still lied.

"Right, we'll go back there tomorrow and give it back."

"No you can't Dad," I nearly shouted, "you can't, I mean they won't be there, they were moving stuff out." Somehow the lies were getting bigger and bigger, but I knew I had to keep Dad away from Lone Farm. If we turned up there the Good Folk were bound to think I'd talked, and I didn't want to be eaten!

Dad nodded but I'm not sure he believed me, "Okay but never again. You hear me, never again." Gertrude started on the third turn. "I guess I owe you twenty quid then," he said, as we pulled away.

I tried to smile but the guilt of lying was heavy on my heart, and the roll of money in my jeans might as well have been hot lead. It was awful; being around the Good Folk had not made me a better person.

Chapter 11

The next day I stuck with Dad all the way through the milk-round from beginning to end. But it wasn't much fun. The weather didn't help; it was one of those days when people say the weather can't make up its mind; which means the weather has decided to be awful. Fits of rain and then moments of sunshine, cold and windy spells, followed by more rain. Not terrible, but also not the best weather to be out on a milk float.

I collected two more 'No more milk please' notes and then slipped over and dropped two bottles. One broke so we had to clear that up; it was just one of those days. Dad tried to be cheerful for my sake, but I could see it was a struggle for him, and before long he stopped singing and the jokes stopped, and I knew exactly where his thoughts had drifted to, to the same place mine were at; how would Mum be when we got there?

The hospice itself was not an unpleasant place, it really wasn't. It was clean and the colours were bright, and everyone was friendly and knew our names. They asked about school and what I was doing for the holidays, but none of that changed why I was there. My Mum was dying, and her illness had changed my life and her going would change my world.

Mum's room was the third room on the right after the reception area, I'll never forget that; we walked in, and the big window was open with its curtains drawn back. And there was Mum, sitting up smiling, her face shining in the sunlight. I was on that bed and hugging her before I knew what I was doing.

Mum kissed Dad and they sat there holding hands, all chat and smiles. Mum even had the strength to moan about Dad's shirt not being ironed, and she told me I needed a haircut, it was incredible. I hadn't seen her that well, that happy in ages. I can't remember everything we talked about, but it felt like we talked about everything and for a while the hospice just melted away. We could have been back home or out on a picnic or anywhere. It didn't matter where we were or why we were there and then Mum grew more serious.

"I've been thinking, and I've decided that when I'm gone, I want to be cremated. I want you and your dad to take my ashes and put them somewhere that reminds you of me, somewhere with happy memories, so that, if you do go back there, you'll think of me in a happy way. I want you to remember the good times we had." There was no fear in her voice, no trace of doubt, she had made up her mind. I wish I could say I shared some of the peace Mum seemed to be feeling but all I felt was cheated and angry. Why did she have to talk about such stuff when we were feeling so good? It wasn't fair! I jumped off the bed and stormed out of the room. I heard Dad calling my name, but I wasn't stopping, I stomped past the reception desk and out of the hospice.

A long bank of earth lined with a thin avenue of Ash trees separated the hospice from the regular hospital, I ran into them and gave one poor tree a good kicking, and when I was done, I put my back against it and just cried my eyes out. I cried so much I couldn't breathe through my snotty nose. I wiped my face on my t-shirt and looked out over the hospital that was spread out below me. I saw an old man dressed in leather shorts jogging towards me.

It was the old man I'd seen at the superstore, he was incredibly thin, and his long grey hair and beard, almost reached his incredibly short brown leather shorts. I heard a shout and then two men and a woman, dressed in white uniforms came running after him. They grabbed hold of his arms and turned him round and led him back the way he'd come, he didn't resist, there was no fight or struggle, in fact the old man laughed, then turned and shouted, "Greetings Bottle, it is I the Wodwo!"

Wodwo? I had no idea what that was, but could it be that I had seen the Green Man?

I did go back in to see Mum, but she was feeling tired by then, I said I was sorry but both Mum and Dad told me not to be, it was okay, they understood, and that helped a bit. Dad and I stopped for fish and chips on the way home, and sat in Gertrude, eating them in silence. We were all talked out and I really didn't mind. It's what people call a comfortable silence. When we'd both licked the vinegar and grease off our fingers, we set off again, and it really was getting dark, but Dad didn't take us home. We drove out of the town and through a village or two and then up this winding road that takes you to the top of the hill that looks over the town. We pulled up in the layby and got out.

Below us lay the orange glow of the town. I knew, if it were light, we'd be able to see village churches and the fields surrounding the town, but now they were just stretches of deep blackness, an emptiness filled with the unseen. You see, I knew the view well, we'd often stopped there; me, Mum and Dad, it was one of our favourite places. Just a place to stop and look and wonder at the world. Dad put his hand on my shoulder and nodded to himself; I knew what he was thinking, this would be the place Mum would want to be, this is where her ashes would stay, and I silently agreed.

Chapter 12

I don't really remember getting home that night, perhaps I fell asleep in the car, but I do remember waking up to the sound of scratching at my window. For a while I just lay there, holding the covers tight over my mouth, but then the scratching became tapping and the tapping got louder and louder until it was a loud bang, bang banging; I jumped out of bed and went to the window.

Standing in our back garden was the old man in his leather shorts. When he saw me, he dropped the tree branch he was banging against my window and waved with a big beaming smile, "it is I the Wodwo, and you are Bottle of the contract."

I waved back. He pointed to the back door. I nodded and signaled for him to be quiet. He rubbed his hands together in glee and grinned his big toothy grin back at me. He was still grinning when I reached the backdoor, I checked the time on the kitchen clock, it was ten minutes past three, Dad would be getting up at four.

"What are you doing here?"

"Finding you Bottle, finding you, fortuitous is it not, the very picture," his body was as crooked and knobbly as an old apple tree, but his voice was sweet and light like an old glockenspiel, "very pleased to meet you Bottle. I've heard nothing about you at all, but I am charmed none the less, charmed is the word is it not, well met, well met."

"Please keep your voice down," I whispered loudly through my teeth, "my dad's asleep upstairs."

"Of course, the Pater, of course… do you have any apples?"

"Apples? No, I don't have any apples."

"What a shame," his naked shoulders dropped, "pity, forlorn, and foolish I, lesson, never leave home without one."

"I think we have apple juice."

"Cider?"

"Juice."

"Juice you say. Yes and why shouldn't you? Apples and juice, yes of course, please yes, juice it is then Bottle."

I went to the cupboard and found one of the cartons of juice I took to school with my packed lunch and handed it to the old man. He looked at it in complete bewilderment. I took it off him, cut off the top, poured it into a glass, and put it in his hand. He sniffed, he beamed.

It's a smile I'd like you to imagine, it was vast and shining and looked as if it belonged to a baby, but set in an ancient leathery, warty face covered in a huge tangled grey beard. It was the sort of smile that brightened a room. The old man sipped the drink and licked his lips and stared intently at the glass, "Not the last apple but still, a nice apple. They used to save the last apple for me Bottle but

not anymore, not for a long time," he sipped again, "yes nice, an English apple, russet and gold, with a just a hint of squashed wasp."

There was only one question I needed answering, "Are you the Green Man?"

"No, I am Wodwo, but they call me the Apple Man. The Green Man is human, I am not human,' he giggled, "they thought me human at the human hospital. To think, they thought me human," he snorted and then downed the rest of the apple juice, "yes, very good West Country apples…but not the last. Is there more?"

I got another carton and held it in front of his face.

"Okay, you can have another but you have to tell me why you're here? What do you want?"

"Another," he said pointing a long dirty nail at the carton.

"No! I mean, yes; you can have another one, but first, tell me why you're here. Why did you come here?"

He sat upright in the chair and looked at me as if I'd said the daftest thing he'd ever heard, "You know where Avalon is yes?"

I nodded, "It's behind Lone Farm. I was there yesterday."

"I wasn't, and I do not know," he spoke sadly, "I have lost Avalon. I lost the Isle of Apples. I wish to return but do not know the way," he lent forward, "I am exceeding old Bottle, exceeding old."

"I can see that. Do you want me to take you there?"

"Oh what fortuitous fortitude!" he sang, jumping to his feet.

"Please, be quiet. I'll take you. But not now, we can't leave till later, not until Dad's gone."

"The Pater, I understand," he said with a tap of his nose and a wink, "as you wish Bottle, I am grateful, we shall be as mice waiting for the cat to pass, as quiet as toads," he whispered with a bow.

"Don't you mean as quiet as mice?"

"No, as toads. Mice are not quiet; they chatter like oaks."

I decided doing something was a better course of action than standing there, trying to grasp the Apple Man's riddles, "now we need to hide you." I took hold of his hand and felt the chill of his bones through his rough dry skin, "you're freezing!"

"No more than I should be, its cold outside," he replied as he followed me into the hall and up the stairs, "cold preserves don't you know. But over time it may wrinkle the skin."

We crept across the landing and into my room. I sat him on the bed and as quickly and silently as I could I made space in my cupboard, throwing clothes on the bed and pilling bags and boxes of toys against the walls until there was enough space in there for the Apple Man to sit. He'd be a little squeezed but comfortable enough and more importantly, he'd be out of view. I backed him into the cupboard and kept the door ajar using a shoe box full of marbles.

"You awake?" Dad called as he opened my bedroom door.

"I couldn't sleep," I said sitting up and rubbing my eyes whilst the Apple Man grinned and waved at me from the cupboard.

"Are you coming with me then? This room is a mess," he said casting a slow critical eye over the mess I'd only just created.

"Yeah I know, I thought I'd stay home and tidy up. I've got some homework to catch up on too."

"Still? Better get it done then. Get your head down for a bit then get stuck into this mess later," he disappeared out of the door and a moment later reappeared, "I'm going up to see Mum straight after work, want me to pick you up?"

"Can I meet you there?"

"If you like, but I can just as easily pop back and pick you up. Tell you what, I'll give you a call from there," and off he went again.

The Apple Man was holding his sides and rocking with laughter but to his credit, he didn't make a sound which somehow made him look even more ridiculous. I got up and shut the cupboard door, I had to concentrate. I sat back on the bed and listened until I heard the front door close. The car door slammed, then Gertrude's ignition screamed three times, her engine spluttered into life, and then after a screechy gear change, she finally pulled away.

I jumped up and pulled on a t-shirt, jumper and jeans, then threw open the cupboard door, grabbed the Apple Man's icy hands and pulled him to his feet.

"Wait there!" I said as firmly as I could, "I need to find you some clothes."

"Why?" he asked, wide-eyed.

"It's cold, and you're nearly naked… and as you say, you're exceedingly old. I can't have you catching cold, and we'll look less suspicious going across the estate if you're dressed."

"Crafty young Bottle, very crafty," he said tapping his long misshapen nose, "a true son of Adam, but tell me, how does one catch the cold?"

I went into Mum and Dad's room and grabbed some clothes from Dad's drawer, and an old coat from the back of the closet and ran back into my room. The Apple Man was bouncing energetically on my bed, laughing like a gleeful toddler.

"Will you pack it in!" I shouted. He stopped bouncing and sat on the edge of the bed, smiling like a naughty three-year-old. It was difficult to be angry with him, but I was getting there.

I'd never had to help anybody to get dressed before, and it's not as easy as you think. And trying to dress someone who's extremely ticklish, and only ever wears leather shorts doesn't make it any easier, but we got it done, after much protest, laughter and struggle. The Apple Man's feet were massive, easily as broad as my hand, and about long as my forearm, there was no way any of the shoes in our house were going to fit him.

"We'll just have to risk it, I guess," I said.

"Fortune flavours the cider," the Apple Man pronounced.

"Let's hope so," I sighed, as I led him down the stairs, and out of the house.

I really shouldn't have worried about people seeing us, it was still the time of day that only milkmen and postmen see. But trying to get across the estate with Apple Man was a job and a half. Firstly, he had a very strange way of walking. It wasn't really a walk more of a slow lolloping skip. Those big feet gave him a huge advantage as one of his strides was worth two of mine. Sometimes I had to run just to keep up, especially when he thought he smelled an apple tree in someone's garden. Off he'd go, crisscrossing from house to house, sniffing and then licking his lips until I dragged him away, and then he'd lollop on for a while until he smelled another tree.

I knew I had to speed things up, at the rate we were going; we were likely to bump into Dad on his milk round, and I really didn't want to have that conversation! Somehow, I had to keep the Apple Man's mind on the job or perhaps, it would be wiser if his mind was somewhere else, and his feet were moving forward.

"So how did you leave Avalon?" I asked, linking my arm into his, and dragging him away from another front garden.

"To find another Wodwo, or the last apple, or perhaps the Green Man. I forget, I am exceeding old."

"You know I thought you might have been the Green Man, I've been looking for him too."

He looked at me and then patted me on the head, "Do not trouble your head child. Our ways are not your ways."

I don't know if it was the situation, or too many early mornings and late nights, but I was suddenly very annoyed. I let go of his arm and stood there with my arms folded, fuming. I waited for him to realise I wasn't walking with him – it took another four strides – and then he turned to face me, "what ails thy Bottle?"

"I wish people would stop calling me child. I know what I am I don't need to be reminded."

"Are you sure of that? It seems humans have forgotten an awful lot."

"It's about time someone explained something to me. I understand your ways are not our ways, believe me I get it. But I do have questions! And that might not be your way, but it is mine, and I need to understand what's going on. If you have a story, I'd like to hear it."

The Apple Man gathered his long beard into his hand and peered into it as if he expected to find a bug in its twisted mass, which wouldn't have surprised me at all; "it is a passing strange request Bottle. The past can't be visited even by those who have lived it, and I am exceeding old Bottle," he held out his hand to me, "your kind's need to understand is a strange sickness, I cannot cure it."

"I don't want it cured! I just want to understand! Can you tell me about Avalon?"

"That I can tell you, for I planted Avalon," he pushed his long gnarly fingers into his hair and scratched violently, "I shall tell but I cannot explain. The life is mine. Your understanding is your own," he took his hands from his hair, plunged them deep into the coat pockets, and began his tale in a lilting singsong voice.

The Apple Man's Tale

(As it was told to me – as best as I can recall)

Wodwo, Wodwo me, my mother was a bud, my father was a bee, busy being, they had much work for me. I was to walk the earth, friend to the bees, planting the whole world with apple trees. All alone, walking free, more than a man, less than a tree, wandering the world, planting seeds, Wodwo, Wodwo me.

Soon lovely saplings growing everywhere. Winters, summers came and went, the world was full of blossoms scent, but I didn't rest, I went further, farther, to and fro, on and on through rain and snow, till one spring my feet began to slow, I was cowered, bent, knobbly and old. But still on I went all alone, wandering the world, planting seeds, Wodwo, Wodwo me.

Wodwo, Wodwo me, always sow in hope, planting, weeding, forgive the disappointing season, moving on, forever leaving my loved ones growing. Years of digging and toiling, preparing the ground, but never knowing which would grow, no brothers to play with, no sisters to tease… on I went, wandering the world, planting seeds, Wodwo, Wodwo me.

Wodwo, Wodwo me, reached a rich and gentle land, with no more than a handful of seeds in my hand, the sea sneaked in behind my back, I was cut off, trapped! I had nothing but time and my skill, so I planted the seeds on the crest of a hill. I sat and watched the saplings grow and soon I'd grown an apple grove but here was mystery, something I did not know, something was living far below, Wodwo, Wodwo me.

Wodwo, Wodwo me, busy as a bee, the fruit was good, soon the grove was a mighty wood, then came a cold Autumnal night, I heard singing and saw dancing lights. The people of the Hollow Hills, celebrating the chill, came dancing out. I gave them gifts of fruit, and they ate their fill, they gave me everything I lacked, love and roots, they gave more than I could ever pay back. No more alone, happy me, they named this Wodwo, now Apple Man me.

We lived happily in this land, the Isle of Apples, Avalon in Albion, land of rain and misty shore, land of trees and apple cores. Then men came from across the seas, they brought their own cultivated trees, cousins and sons to my own apple trees. These were apples I had never met from places I had once known, and the thought came to me, could there be somewhere a Mrs Wodwo, Wodwo Apple Tree?

I travelled the whole world checking every tree, mixing and matching pollen and seeds. Man planting orchards in straight lines for apple cider and apple wine. But naughty man discarded the misshapen fruit which were by rights mine, I told them leave them be, for the strangest fruit may grow into one Wodwo, Wodwo, like me.

But man does not listen or does not care, he builds and ploughs everywhere, so I haunted orchards on the moonless nights, to give him a fright, I'd snatch him up and give him a wallop and a thump! I'd bang his head and bash his knees, for being a bully and boxing the trees. I stopped the apples, told them not to grow and men wept in the apple grove… I was angry, then I was sad, my search had turned me from Wodwo good, to Wodwo bad.

I sought a bargain for the good of all, even though man is crafty, he still has a right to live here too, and so it was agreed that as payment for the fruit of my trees, man would sing a Wassailing Song and leave the last apple from every tree for me, and should a tree ever sing along to their Wassailing Song, man would leave that tree alone, and send for me, for that would be my Mrs Wodwo, Wodwo Apple Tree.

I thought the deal good, honest and fair, but man thinks too much and loses his hair, a careless thing I'll think you'll agree, if man forgets his hair, he's bound to forget what he swears. The deal was broken long ago but we who are not flesh and bone, we remember and my search goes on…but now… Wodwo, Wodwo alone."

The Apple man stopped and looked at the ground and seemed to sway on his massive feet as he lent on Lone Farm's five bar gate for support.

"I am alone and wish to go home," the Apple Man coughed, as he looked up to the sky, and fell at my feet.

Chapter 13

The Apple Man wasn't breathing, and even under his leather brown tan I could see that his skin was paling. I threw the gate open and hitched him up on my back, piggyback style and began carrying him down the drive. Three steps in and I was wet with sweat and buckling at the knees. I couldn't believe how heavy the skinny old man was and his huge feet were acting like anchors dragging on the seabed, I wasn't going to make it. I laid him down on the drive and ran the rest of the way. The front door opened wide before I reached it and I jumped through, screaming; "Help! The Apple Man is sick."

The door at the far end of the hall flew open and Thorn stood there glaring. He leapt over my head and raced out the door; a breath later he was running back up the corridor with the Apple Man in his arms. I ran after him through the kitchen, and out the back door. Thorn was already leaping along Haggis Hop. As soon as he reached the other side he threw the Apple Man to the floor, tore off the clothes, and began covering his whitening skin, with great handful of grass and dirt.

By the time I reached them, the Apple Man was almost completely buried, with only his grey face visible. I didn't know what to do, so I grabbed a handful of grass, and yelled, "what do I do?"

"Put it in his mouth!" Thorn yelled back at me.

I looked at the muddy roots in my hand, "do what?"

"Put it in his mouth!"

The Apple Man's mouth was slack but closed. I shut my eyes, took hold of his beard, yanked it down, and stuffed the grass deep into his mouth.

Thorn sat back against one of the standing stones and rubbed his hands together, picking mud from his fingernails, "why was he wearing clothes, they cut him off from the sun. Did you do this to him?"

"I didn't know... it was cold."

"Have you ever seen a tree shiver?" Thorn snarled.

"I didn't know," I protested, "what's going to happen?"

"That depends on what will happen."

I nodded in agreement, perhaps I was getting used to the Good Folk's babbling, "I saw him at the superstore, and then yesterday at the hospital, and then..."

"A what?"

"A hospital, you know, it's where people go if they're ill or need looking after...."

"Was he sick?" Thorn interrupted.

"No, I don't think so, but he was very old."

"Old is not ill," Thorn said in disgust.

"But sometimes old people get frail and need looking after."

"So they take you from the land that gives life and put you in a building away from the living sun… what a wonderful breed you are."

"It's not so bad. They give you apple crumble," grinned the Apple Man, sitting up with a start, "I'm covered in mud… how lovely!"

Before I had time to think I was hugging the hairy, muddy old man. Thorn stood, brushed the last traces of earth from his gown and took hold of the Apple Man's hands, pulling him to his feet.

"Welcome home, Apple Man, we have missed you."

"You have been away too long," the Crone said, appearing from behind the stones, "too long searching for your foolish dream. And to no avail, I'm sure," she said roughly instantly turning into the beautiful woman, "welcome home my love," this said, she turned into the little girl, "welcome home my Lord," she said with a smile as she took the Apple Man's hand and turned back into the beautiful dark-haired woman.

"Morgana my love," the Apple Man's voice cracked as he fell to his knees and then kissed the woman's hand, "forgive me."

"I always do and always shall, for I know your heart is true, come now gather your strength," saying this, she took the old man's face in her hands and kissed his lips – for a long time, a very long time.

As I tried not to watch, the Apple Man's leathery skin changed colour, a mottled green wash flowed from his skin and into his hair and beard. His skin was no longer dry and old but was full and fresh, as if it had taken on the appearance of a firm ripe apple. I could see he was still incredibly old and gnarled but he looked strong and full of life. He looked at me and smiled, and that smile had not changed; it was still the biggest baby grin I had ever seen.

"Thank you Morgana," he bowed to the young woman, who turned into the Crone, who gave his beard a sharp yank. "And I thank you my lady." He then turned to me and bowed, "And thanks also to you Bottle,"

"No don't, I made you wear clothes, I could have killed you."

"No Bottle, you brought me home and I thank you," he turned to the Crone, "did you know Bottle would find me?"

"No, I had no hand in it. You have done well Bottle and…" she gestured to Thorn, and he stepped forward, "as always, our thanks to you, mighty Thorn. Are we agreed that Bottle has lived up to his side of the contract?"

"So far," Thorn said sharply.

"We agree then, he should be rewarded for this act," she smiled.

Thorn bowed reluctantly as he shot me a glare.

The Crone turned back into Morgana – which of course was only one of the Crone's many names – flicked a lump of earth from the Apple Man's beard, kissed his cheek, and then whispered very loudly so all could hear, "Bottle has yet to see Avalon, and there are apples in the grove awaiting you, perhaps you would like to show them to him, it seems fitting."

"How pleasant that would be," the Apple Man sighed and knelt before me, "come Bottle let us see the apples of Avalon together. Climb on my back."

I was suddenly very conscious of the time, it was still pretty early but I couldn't let myself lose track, let Dad down and miss seeing Mum again, "sorry but I can't be late today. I really should get going."

The air around me was filled by a hundred invisible laughs.

The Apple Man smiled kindly. "Bottle I give you my word. I shall have you back home before you need to be. You have brought me home, trust me to return the kindness. Climb on my back Bottle."

"No I don't think so, I'll hurt you."

"Hurt me how?"

"You are very old."

"Exceeding old indeed, but to refuse would hurt me more," he said calmly.

He bent down low, and I wrapped my arms around his neck and shoulders. His arms hoisted me up and gripped my legs as he slowly stood, shaking a little at the knees.

"Are you sure you can carry me?" I whispered into his hair, "I don't mind if you can't. I don't want you to hurt yourself."

Once again, the air filled with laughter.

"Quiet yourself," the Apple Man's voice was clear and strong, "I am the root and the core. I am the branch and the seed. I am the fruit and the branch and the tree...I am Wodwo."

"Wodwo!" the unseen voices chorused.

"I am one with wood and tree!"

"Wodwo! Wodwo!" came the echoing chant, growing louder and louder, "Wodwo! Wodwo!"

I could feel his back straighten, the muscles beneath his green skin swell, and his arms and neck thicken. I was raised higher and higher as his already long legs stretched and grew, until they finally fitted his feet. I held on tight.

"I am Wodwo!" he shouted, "the Apple Man."

The answering cheer was lost in the rush of air and speed as we leapt over the standing stones and raced down the hill. My bones rattled as we hurtled forward. I felt like a shaken ragdoll, it was all I could do to hold on.

Avalon was a blur of changing shades of green. Trees were bent out of shape and their leaves torn from their branches as we sped past. The smaller, slower Good Folk were caught up in our wake, twisted about and thrown into the air. They of course loved it, and we were soon surrounded by tiny, winged creatures singing and laughing, surfing the apple Man's jet stream, as we cut through Avalon.

Faster and faster we sped, outrunning the Good Folk, outrunning the fastest bird. Out across a silver lake like a skipping stone we went and then tore on, deep into the reverberating shadows of quivering trees. The Apple Man dodged and ducked, jumped over and around bushes, never faltering never slowing; and then it happened - I looked over his shoulder and thwack! Some luckless fly or wasp hit the back of my throat and I gagged, I reached for my throat, lost my grip, and fell backwards into nothingness.

I actually landed in a patch of nettles – that weren't Nettle – but stung just as badly – and by the time I found my feet, the Apple Man was long gone and there was nothing to show his passing but a swirl of leaves. If I hadn't been jumping up and down in pain, I would have kicked myself for trusting the word of the Good Folk, what a fool! There I was, stranded and in the middle of a wood with a bruised bum and a neck full of nettle stings!

Chapter 14

The wood was dark and damp. I could see patches of blue grey sky, but very little sun made its way through to ground level. Everything seemed to be hiding in the shadow and tangle of itself. I set off at a hobbled pace, trying to follow a straight line, but it was impossible. The thickets were too thick, the brambles too dense and sharp to break through. If I'd been turned around twice on myself, I wouldn't have known it; and I probably was, many times over. I was soon tired, thirsty and hungry. My bruised bum made every step ache and the stinging in my neck had spread to my throbbing ears. A twig snapped under my foot, so loudly it made me jump and then I heard voices. Strange rasping voices, they weren't talking English but somehow, I knew what they were saying, it was an argument, a debate and it sounded very complicated, full of words like 'protocol' and phrases like 'in relation to the aforementioned matter.' I could see a bright patch of light up ahead which meant there was a clearing, I headed for it and then something jumped into my path.

"Go no further if you value your life," it said coldly.

I stood still.

The thing in the shadows also stood still. I waited, and it waited.

"Well?" it said.

"Well what?" I replied.

"Don't you want to go on?"

"You told me to stop," I said.

"And you're going to listen to me?" the figure stepped forward into a dim ray of light; it was the hare I'd met at the gate a few days before, "where's your spirit of adventure child?"

"Don't call me child rabbit!" I snapped.

"Rude!" The hare sniffed, jumping up on its long hind legs, and punching me on the nose. I fell to the floor, my eyes smarting and then my poor bum really protested, I lay on my side and howled like an unhappy dog.

"Oh come on, I didn't hit you that hard," said the hare, sounding very annoyed.

"No, it's my bum! I fell off the Apple Man and landed on my bum."

"So, he's back is he? Returned from his fruitless wandering at last," said the Hare, both his ears pricking up, "how very intriguing. Come now Bottle, do stop whining or the tree council will hear you, and then we'll both be for it."

I stood up as carefully as I could although every step was agony, "Is that the voices I can hear? Is that trees?"

"You can hear them?" he said in surprise, "the Good Folk did a job on you didn't they. I can only barely hear them myself and I'm a hare. Not a rabbit," he added for good measure.

"Aren't you one of the Good Folk?"

The hare looked at me with the look I often seemed to get around the Good Folk, that sort of quizzical 'are you really that stupid' look, "No, as I said I'm a hare, not some silly fairy."

"Then how come you can talk?"

"Perhaps the question should be how come you understand me?" it stepped forward, stood high on its legs and sniffed my face, "some silly fairy magic no doubt."

"Do you have a name then?"

"We don't have names we have scents. I am a servant of Eoster, the May Queen, as are all of my race. We await her return. And that is enough for any human to know," he turned and with three bounding strides reached a boulder that stood just before the last ring of trees that encircled the clearing. He turned to me and beckoned. I took a stiff step forward. The hare coughed and with twitching ears signaled for me to get down, I obeyed and crawled the rest of the way which I have to admit was a lot less painful than walking.

"Not a sound now Bottle our very lives depend upon it," the hare whispered. Slowly we lifted our heads to peak over the boulder.

Ahead of us was a bright grassy clearing, filled with a carpet of mauve bluebells. At its centre was a large pond and gathered around it, with their feet – perhaps I should say roots – resting in the water were twelve figures. Twelve wooden, tree-like figures. To describe them is difficult because they were all different, some were almost human in shape but too tall with too many arms, others were just trees but very much alive and moving. Some were in bud, some were covered in foliage. They communicated their strange dry formal talk by creaking or shaking their branches and rubbing them together at varying speeds – it was an incredibly complex language, and yet I understood every word.

"I would respectfully remind the delegated members that the correct procedure is for the minutes of the last meeting, to be agreed upon as read before proceeding with new items on the agenda that were previously agreed to be discussed in this meeting at the last meeting. All other matters arising should be discussed in new matters arising, if there are any new matters arising which I doubt," a very shiny holly bush stated with a long drawn-out creak and rattle of its spiky leaves.

"We are not questioning the procedure or procedural matters here but merely trying to ascertain what the previous minutes of the last meeting actually said;" a Hazel tree said in a exasperated groan.

"Did the last meeting conclude that we should have recorded minutes?" rasped a Willow.

"Did the last meeting conclude?" asked a most elegant Silver Birch.

"That would be a new matter!" the Holly insisted.

"No, it is an old matter!" complain an Elder tree.

"It is of no matter!" a very sad looking Elm creaked weakly.

They all fell into silence.

The hare slumped back behind the boulder and began cleaning his ears, "And so it goes on," he said with a sigh.

"What on earth are they talking about?" I asked him.

"I have no idea and I don't think they do either. The trouble with tree spirits is that they are very old, very proud and very, very competitive. Every foot of ground every drop of water is fought over. I don't think they could agree even if they wanted to and they just love the sound of their own voices. This meeting has been going on for days!"

"I see," I said, although I'm sure I didn't, "it sounds very important whatever it is… but why are we hiding from trees."

The hare glanced back over the boulder. "I can tell you why I'm here. The water in the pond, that lovely, lovely water. We need it! The animals of Avalon, we all need it! But we can't get to it! Not until they're asleep! And they don't fall asleep until they've talked themselves to sleep. It's always the same, they talk, decide nothing and we're sitting here as parched as sundried worms. It makes my ears hurt."

"I can imagine," and I really could, "but why are hiding?"

"Have you ever been punched by a tree? I can't recommend it. Splat! Splat! Splat!" the Hare exclaimed, thumping the ground with his big left foot, "they are very strong, very bad tempered, proud, vain, boring creatures!" and with that said he blew his whiskers and crossed his ears with an angry shrug.

I looked back over the stone and sure enough the tree spirits were still at it, but as I looked harder, I could also see, shadows moving along the edge of the trees. I could just make out the outline of a deer, and then another, and then a fawn and its mother standing beside a very large hairy pig hiding under a thorn bush. Looking even closer I could see, voles and water rats peaking from behind fallen twigs and half buried stones. All waiting for the trees to sleep, and no doubt all were very thirsty.

"Right!" I said, "I'm not having this, I'll sort them out." I stood up, brushed myself down and began hobbling into the circle of trees.

"You'll get splatted!" the hare warned.

"Don't worry hare," I said over my shoulder, "the Good Folk have signed a contract that will keep me safe."

"But…" the hare shouted, "they're not Good Folk, they're trees!"

By the time the hare's cautionary words had sunk in, it was too late, I was already in the clearing.

"Human!" a willow trees screamed with the snapping of twigs, "Burner! Sapling killer! Tree Feller!"

Something rough and sinewy grabbed me around the waist and a moment later I was dangling upside down, surrounded by angry yelling trees.

"Pull him apart! Give his blood to the earth! Food! Make fertilizer out of his bones!" they went on, "snap him in two! Squish him… slowly!"

"Now then, hold on a minute," I said, "is this any way to treat an official delegation?"

The trees seemed to look at each other for guidance.

"I don't know, is it?" asked the Oak.

"Probably not," replied a Beech tree.

I was quickly placed back on my feet, "whose delegate are you?" a Hawthorne tree enquired, poking me with a very sharp twig.

I gave myself another brush down, and cleared my throat as the trees leant in to hear me speak, "I represent the animals of Avalon," I said, as firmly as I could.

"Those that scurry?" the Ash said so sharply it sounded as if a branch had been broken.

"Do they have a delegation?" the Holly asked, "are they affiliated?"

"They must be, because I'm here," I said with us much conviction as I could muster.

The trees all groaned in unison and nodded their top branches in begrudging agreement.

"So the thing is…" I shut my eyes and pictured all the boring speeches I'd ever had to sit through when Dad was watching the news, "my members, those that scurry wish to come to this pond, in order to partake, in these waters…to drink in order to survive which is their right as animals of Avalon!"

I heard a tiny cheer from the edge of the clearing; I think it was a Hedgehog.

"This is our water," the Oak tree creaked as it shook a branch in my face.

"We were here first," the Silver Birch insisted, "our roots are as deep as our thirst."

"And our thirst is deep," the Willow chimed in.

"I'm sure that's true but their thirsts are very small, we'd take so little, you'd not miss any," I said.

"We shall not share with flesh and bone," Rowan shook angrily.

"But my members thirsts are very small and…and we…" The words were getting away from me again. I knew what I wanted to say but I just didn't have the words, I'm sure you know the feeling. I recalled a very red-faced man I'd seen shouting on the news and how he'd taken on the reporter who was giving him a hard time. I walked up to the oak and pushed my finger into its bark and shouted; "Industrial action! If our demands are not met, we will resort to industrial action. I'm calling a strike!"

The trees shook with fear and exclaimed; "A strike!"

"Can he do that now?" Holly rustled.

"Man is clever he may have learned," Oak quivered.

"Man can call fire from the sky!" Willow wailed.

Tree language is very old and its words are dry and inflexible with each word has a particular meaning. Although I'd said strike they'd heard 'lightning'. I realised their mistake and decided to make the most of it.

"Yes I could do that…I can call a strike."

"He'll use industrial action!" the Oak thrashed.

"Why would you harm us human? We are the air bringers," the Willow wept.

"To kill one of us is to kill our kind," Hazel said, shaking in terror, "to wipe us from the world."

"And some of us are very weak, depleted, not long for this world!" the Elm cried.

"Please I wish you no harm. I am Bottle of the Contract. I give you my word, there shall be no strike! But my members must be allowed to come and go freely without fear of harm."

The trees rattled in discomfort at the thought.

"Man always talks in threats and never keeps his word," the Elm quivered.

Fear only gets you so far, it's much more effective to tempt than it is to threaten. I had to sweeten the medicine, "Of course, what my members really wish, is to be near such wise and learned creatures. They have no council of their own you see. They wish to learn, to watch and learn and drink with you as brothers in Avalon… to form another committee of…things."

"Another committee?" the Holly tree said brightly, "we have time for another committee...of course it would entail a whole new set of protocols."

"The meetings would be interminable," Ash creaked, "never-ending meetings…how marvelous!"

"And you'd need subcommittees and even…um…select committee hearings?" I added even though I had no idea what I was saying.

"Select committees!" they cheered.

"Shall we vote?" the Holly asked lifting one branch high into the air; the clearing was filled with a rattling roar of; "motion carried!"

"We agree," a twisted old Yew tree growled, "that your members may come and witness our sittings and there will be fresh protocols and standards and so much more for them to witness…and in the process of their education they may drink at the water to sustain their learning."

"We are agreed Bottle," Oak exclaimed with such joy that new budding leaves burst out all over him, "its historic! It is historic! We have never agreed on anything before!"

"And for our part I agree that we shall call no strikes," I placed my hand on my heart for emphasis, "of course I can't speak for the independent thunderstorms."

"That is understood," said the Elm. "Thor is not part of our agreement."

"Agreed, long may the council of committees live…and grow." I took hold of the Oaks branch and shook it firmly. Unfortunately, he shook back, and I flew across the clearing and fell on my back.

"I do apologise," the Oak groaned, "one forgets one's own formidable strength."

"It's Okay. Don't worry…ouch," I winced. I couldn't move. Everything hurt.

"Bruised bum is it?" twitched the Hare.

"Very."

The hare stood up on its toes and shouted, "Hampshire! Hampshire! Over here if you please."

A very large hairy pig with tiny dark eyes appeared from the trees. It stood over me with his hot piggy breath in my face. His snout snuffled into my hair and then he sneezed, spraying piggy snot all over me, "Allergies," it snorted.

The hare introduced us in a very polite manner, "Bottle this is Hampshire Hog, Hampshire, Bottle of the Contract."

Hampshire snuffled up a long string of sticky snot and twitched his ears. A warm piggy greeting to be sure.

"We need to get him to Sulis. He's injured and needs to take the waters," said the hare.

"No I don't! Do I? I need to find Apple Man."

"My dear Bottle, without Sulis' help you won't reach the edge of the wood, let alone find the Apple Man."

"Visit Sulis and she will heal you. You swear by Sulis' waters don't you Hampshire?"

"Allergies," Hampshire snorted.

"Hampshire will take you there. He's very strong and knows the way," the Hare jumped off my chest and pushed himself under my shoulder, "he doesn't say much but he's a decent hog as hogs go."

Hampshire lowered his head and with a shove or two from Hare I managed to pull myself onto his hard wiry back.

"Perhaps you could treat Hampshire to a session whilst you're there?" the hare added with a wink, "if you have some coins or gifts on you?"

I'd heard him but I wasn't paying attention at that point, "Is it far?"

"Not as the hog hops," the hare laughed as it waved us off.

Chapter 15

Hampshire's back was wide but hard as rock and his skin was tight, dry and flaky and there was nothing to hold onto but the course wiry hairs that covered his back, and he didn't like you holding onto those. He made that very clear straight off with a sharp squeal. And what do you say to a pig? I was sore, bruised and hungry and all I could think about was bacon sandwiches. I remember thinking that I must have eaten a cousin or an uncle of Hampshire's and I'm sure Hampshire was thinking the same thing too; so on we went in polite but awkward conversation...

"Nice tree," I'd say.

Snort.

"Lovely weather."

Snort.

"Are we there yet?"

Snort.

I gave up.

Eventually, the ground around us became boggy and uneven, the earth oozed, sucked and squelched and even Hampshire found it hard going, and then without warning, Hampshire stopped and sat down with a, "Snort."

"Are we there? Is this it?"

Hampshire squealed loudly, and a very small man emerged out of a half-submerged tree trunk. His skin was as red as the mud that oozed from the straggly grass at his feet, and his body was covered in bumps, lumps, warts and patches of moss, but nothing else. He was a very lumpy, muddy, naked little man. He looked me up and down, scratched his fat belly and sniffed his fingers, "Good to see you Hampshire, the usual is it?"

"Allergies," Hampshire snorted.

The little man looked me over again, "First time is it? Course it is, never forget a face me," the dumpy little man said, with a wink. "Hold on a minute me loves," and shouted over his shoulder, "right then, you 'orrible lot! We've got customers. Get moving!"

Suddenly the patch of grass behind him stood up, divided into a hundred different clumps and walked off into the trees. Now there was a large round muddy hole in the centre of the clearing where the grass had been.

"That's amazing. What are they?" I asked.

"Thank you very much, that is stray grass, and I trained it myself," he sniffed proudly, "and you are Bottle are you not."

"I am. And you are Bog."

"Yes, Bog by name and bog by nature, that's me. Do you come with an offering? A gift for Sulis?"

"Sorry a what?" I spluttered.

"A gift for Sulis, as way of payment."

"I see, yes of course," I recalled what the hare had said and started searching my pockets, "and one for Hampshire too please, on me, if that's all right?"

"Not a problem, but that would obviously depend on the offering," Bog grinned, "so what you got?"

I held out both hands. I had four ten pence pieces, a role of twenty-pound notes, some sweet wrappers, a red elastic band and a blue centred glass marble.

"The paper monies no good here, I know where it's been. But the coins are good and the red thing's nice, but I reckon the glass eye seals the deal. Now, here's the thing," Bog bent over and picked up a handful of wet sodden earth, "I know this stuff is mud, you know it's mud, we all know it's mud, but to Sulis, this is the finest cleanest spring water in the whole world, and we want Sulis to be happy, don't we? So, there is no mud. You get me, just pure clean spring water," he winked.

I didn't get it at all, but I nodded.

"Nice. One other thing, the Romans, don't mention those swine, sorry Hampshire," he added with another wink, "don't mention the Romans and if she offers you lavender, say no, you don't like it. Are we clear? Good, then make your offering to Sulis, Queen of the Springs."

"Do what?"

"Throw it in the mud."

I threw the offering into the mud.

"Sulis, oh Sulis," Bog sang out, in a huge booming voice that was far too large and tuneful for his knobbly little body, "oh Sulis, sweet, sweet Sulis my lady... come on out 'ere now, or so help me I'll cut this grass to stubble."

The mud bubbled. At first just here and there around the edges and then more quickly with bigger and louder plops until the mud hole was gurgling and spluttering like a glass of chocolate milkshake blown by unseen giant straws.

Just then a thought popped into my head so just had to ask, "Why no lavender?"

Bog looked at the bubbling mud in alarm and shushed me, then whispered, "Roman aren't it, don't mention the Romans. Got it!"

"Got it...."

"Be still mortal," Bog commanded in a very showy voice, "for Queen Sulis approaches!"

The bubbling mud began twisting around as if it were about to go down a giant plughole, but instead of going down, it went up into the air and formed a huge spinning spout. At first the top of the spout swung about, dropping and swooping, like a great lolling tongue, Then, as it spun faster and faster, it grew longer and longer, as it tightened itself into a funnel and then into a sharp muddy spike, that collapsed back in on itself with a resounding plop. Standing in the centre of the pool of mud was a tall redheaded woman, dressed in a faded green tartan shawl and a long mud splattered indigo dress; although, both of these were almost entirely hidden by her incredibly long, incredibly red hair.

"Welcome weary travelers," she said, in a light bubbling voice, "I see our good friend Hampshire has returned, you are most welcome." Hampshire snorted and without a moment's hesitation walked into the mud and sunk up to his neck, he was one happy pig. "This is a face I do not know? Tell me Bog, who is this weary traveler? Please introduce our guest," Sulis said with the sweetest smile.

"This is Bottle, oh Sulis, beautiful Sulis Queen of the spring. Oh Sulis would you honor him with your healing touch?" Bog stared up at her, his big fat eyes full of love.

"You are most welcome, all are welcome, the waters of healing are for all," she burbled warmly, "tell me Bottle, what ails thee?"

I couldn't say a word, not a word. I just couldn't talk to her; she was too lovely, too perfect to burden with my problems. Bog pulled on my arm. I bent down and whispered into his ear.

"He has a bruised bum!" Bog shouted and I nearly died of shame.

"Poor thing, come to the spring Bottle, come to the healing waters of Sulis and be well, let your bum be whole."

Bog snorted. I ignored him, bowed and made my way to the mud.

"Oi! What's your game then?" Bog said, blocking my path, "no clothes, house rules."

"No clothes, what none at all," I stammered, feeling myself going very red, I didn't like getting changed for sports at school let alone taking all my clothes off in the middle of a strange wood in front of a Bog, a pig and the nicest, sweetest person in the world.

"You can keep your undergarments on if you must," Bog said begrudgingly, "really humans and their bodies, I ask you, what a lot of fuss."

"Be gentle Bog," Sulis said soothingly, "to be modest in an immodest world is no crime."

"You're so right Sulis. So wise," Bog said dreamily as he clapped his hands together. Moments later five flying Good Folk; Myrtle, Mallow, Rush, Reed and Samfer, were buzzing around my head. They whizzed around and around me giggling like tickled babies, until I was dizzy and much to my surprise, almost naked. I wasn't cold, I was too embarrassed. I ran to the mud and jumped in.

The mud was as soft as melted chocolate and just as warm. It hugged like a warm pillow and yes it did sooth my aching bum and stinging neck. It was simply fantastic, not too hot not too cold, just perfectly warm and smooth, utter bliss.

Sulis piled her hair into a towering flame on top of her head, sat down beside me and dabbed a spot of mud across my forehead, "I see you Bottle, I see your pain. What a shame to find so many worries, such a heavy heart in one so young... it breaks my heart."

"Oh I'm alright," I replied, and I meant it, right then and there I didn't have a worry in the world.

"Of course you are," she whispered, gently rubbing more mud into my scalp, "you're very strong, very brave. But to feel fear is no shame. You really do have a lot on your mind don't you?" she drew a muddy stripe across my top lip, "so much tension. So many worries, in one so young. Come lessen your burden. Tell me your worries, what troubles your mind Bottle?"

"Sometimes...my Mum's ill, really ill and it makes me so angry. It's so unfair."

"Of course it is Bottle, of course it is," she sympathised, working a generous dollop of mud into my hair, "but I have something that will help you, something to take away all the worries and fears. To heal your sadness, would you like that Bottle, would you like me to stop all the sadness?"

"Yes please..." I gurgled into the rising mud, as she held her open hand under my nose. Sitting on her palm was a small bright blue frog. I looked at it and it looked at me and rubbed a front leg over one of its eyes as if I wasn't there at all.

"Isn't it pretty Bottle?" Sulis said, "blue as the sky, blue as the spring."

"Lovely blue," I replied.

"Let me help you." She whispered and placed the frog on my head. "Now then Bottle what were we talking about?"

I had to think.

"I don't know…I can't remember."

"Does it matter?" she smiled.

"No probably not…this is nice."

"Yes, this is nice," Sulis confirmed.

"Nice."

"Not this one sweet Sulis no!" Bog insisted.

Sulis put her hands on top of my head, and with the gentlest, sweetest smile, pushed me under the warm, velvet, airless mud.

I didn't panic, I wasn't concerned. The world was warm and dark and filled with silence. The warm wet earth covered me and pressed in on me from all sides. I could feel myself drifting into nothingness.

Something rough and rasping took hold of my foot, worked its way up my leg, and wrapped itself around my waist. There was a rush of movement and noise. I was moving through the mud at incredible speed. The next thing I knew I was flying through the open air. I hit a wall and then landed sprawling, coughing and spitting on a hard floor.

A lot more of coughing, spitting, gasping and wheezing followed. I clawed the mud out of my nose and ears, and tried to figure out where I was; at first I thought it was night time because it was so dark, but I slowly became aware that I was completely surrounded by specks of dim green light moving around in the darkness. I reached out and touched one, it was cold, slimy and most definitely, a worm. I pulled my hand back and watched as the glowing green worms wriggled beside me, before me, above and below me.

Chapter 16

I was in a long narrow tunnel, but thanks to the glowing worms there was enough light to see a few feet ahead but that was all. If a tiger had been waiting to pounce three steps beyond me, I wouldn't have known it was there until I was in its jaws.

Now, in most stories this is the point where the young hero shows their real courage. They roll up their sleeves and get going. Off into the dark they go, regardless of what might be there, well I didn't. This is an honest story, and the truth is I sat down there in the dark and cried my little eyes out. I just couldn't go on. I'd really had enough, and to be honest, despite being older, bigger and wiser today, if I was in the same circumstances; I'm not sure I could do any better. Of course, what I now know is that once you've had a good cry, things tend to look different, and you do somehow just get on with it. Unfortunately, after my good cry I was still nearly naked, bruised, wet and filthy and lost down in a stinking dark tunnel miles away from home.

Sometimes you feel a sound before you really hear it, feel it deep down in your stomach before you know what it is; and I felt the drums before I heard the slow steady drumbeat coming from the darkness. Drums or just one drum I wasn't sure. The sound was bouncing around the walls like a rubber ball. But they were getting closer, much, much closer. There's something about the sound of drums isn't there, something faintly stirring and definitely threatening. Drums tell you an army is coming, and you better watch out. Boom, boom, boom the beat exploded like thunder, but I could hear something else too, higher pitched above the dull thud of the drums, an odd snuffling, shuffling sound. Interspersed with ear piercing disgruntled squeaks. I put my fingers in my ears and strained to see into the darkness but saw nothing until they were nearly on top of me.

"Halt!" shouted the stout little man, whose toy tin drum had nearly collided with my knees. "What are you doing here? What are you?" he demanded, whilst poking me with his drumstick, "are you Elf or Wodwo?"

"No, I'm Bottle, I'm human."

"Oh rot a dead dog!" he shouted, "I thought they'd stopped using kids down the mines," his voice rattled like a pebble in a tin can, "don't you know it's dangerous to block the tunnels?"

I looked into the dim light behind him, and there I saw another two little men. They were all dressed in the same dirty grey clothes with flat caps and square-toed muddy black boots. However, the other two seemed taller but when I looked harder, I could see they were standing on something, something that moved and squealed. I just couldn't make out what it was. The little drummer poked me again and asked, "where are your tools? Where's your lamp? What kind of miner loses his lamp?"

"I'm not a miner."

"I can see that, so what are you doing here?"

"I don't know, I can't remember." I shut my eyes and tried to concentrate on the memory that was waving at me through the shifting waves of fog that filled my head, but I just couldn't see it. But then a feeling rose up from my chest and blow the fog aside, "I'm lost."

"Nah ya not," said the little man with the tin drum with great conviction, "don't talk daft. You're here, so you're fine. If you woz somewhere else, then you'd be lost." He stroked his dirty beard with great pleasure, and then said, "but you ain't. So it's fine, innit."

I must have grown accustomed to the Good Folk babble by then, because that made some kind of sense to me, but I had a problem to solve; "how did I get here?"

"How should I know?" the little man laughed, "but I imagine you fell, most people fall into holes, some jump, some climb but most fall. Others get buried, of course, but they tend to be dead. And you don't look dead. Did you fall?"

"Yes, that's right," I could feel the space in my head left by the fog was beginning to refill, "I fell… from the Apple Man."

The little man shrieked, dropped his drum and jumped for joy; hitting his head on the roof of the tunnel. Then all three of them began running in a tight little circle around the drum, jumping up and down like excited rabbits shouting; "We've done it! We've done it!" When they were too dizzy to dance anymore, they fell on top of me, laughing so hard their faces turned bright blue.

"You've seen the Apple Man!" the man gasped picking up his tin drum.

"I saw him this morning. I think it was this morning. He dropped me, or I fell off…. I can't really remember what happened."

"And you've seen," he paused and licked his bright blue lips, "others!"

"If you mean the Good Folk, yes I have…"

"We've done it lads, we've done it!" he said with his bright blue face getting brighter and brighter. He then snatched the grey flat cap from his head, and slapped it about both his friend's faces. A gesture they instantly returned in kind, with great force and much laughter. This done the three men crowded around me again and pushed their dirty faces close to mine. They were so close I could feel their eyelashes brushing against my cheeks.

"My names Dig, these are my brothers, Dug and that's Ditch," he said, and now that they were so close, I could tell there was no way to tell them apart, they were identical, even down to the smudges of mud on their clothes and faces.

"And what was your name?" they said in unison, "and where are you from? And why are you in our tunnel?"

"My name?" I had to think, "Bottle, and I signed a contract. And I should know who you are but… I can't tell you apart."

"What contracts that then pal, a building contract? A mining contract?" Dig (I think) asked.

I really wasn't sure, "the contract, I am Bottle of the contract! They were going to eat me."

"Who'd want to eat you?" Dug winced.

"Not me," Dig squirmed.

"Nasty," Dug squirmed.

Ditch nodded, and squirmed.

"Very nasty," Dig agreed, "the thing is Bottle, we've been out of touch with Avalon for a while now, and well..."

"But Thorn said," Thorn's cold triangular face jumped into my head, but I couldn't remember exactly what he'd said, "I thought it was magic."

"Thorn! You've met old diamond-eye too have you, now there's a rum one. Is he still telling that story about the three goats? Utter nonsense, I was there. Look Bottle, magic doesn't solve everything. It doesn't build tunnels does it," Dig laughed.

Now that did make sense, my head was definitely clearing, "So, if you don't mid me asking, what are you?"

"Down in Cornwall, your lot called us Knockers or the Coblynau," Dig said, giving Ditch a little shove, "and we dig tunnels. We are very good at tunnels..."

"Love tunnels," Dug confirmed.

Ditch nodded.

"Love 'um," Dig went on, "we used to help out the human miners, we liked that, we liked that a lot. But mining's gone right down these last few years," his dirty little face took on a sadly wistful expression, "and of course they've brought those machines in to do the tunnels in London."

"Not natural is it," Dug complained.

"You know London, you've been to London?" I asked.

"Know it, seen it, dug it," Dug paused, stood back and looked me up and down, "you got no clothes on."

"I know, I can't remember how it happened," as I said this something hit me in the face. It was a grey suit jacket, followed by a pair of trousers and a flat cap and three pairs of shoes, I picked them up and hurriedly put them on. I was very grateful, "thank you, thank you so much; where did you get all this? This isn't from…graves is it?"

"We are not grave robbers." Dig snorted indignantly.

"We found them. We find lots. It's amazing the things people lose on the underground. I swear if I see another umbrella I'll throw-up my own head," Dug laughed.

I pulled on the jacket. It was tight and smelt of old dirt and bad water, but it was better than nothing. I sat down and looked at the shoes, only two were an actual pair, the others were just odd shoes tied together at the laces. The matching pair looked to be a size too large for me, but I decided wearing them was probably better than walking around a stony tunnel in bare feet, "These are really old," I commented when I'd finally managed to lever them on.

"We've been carrying them around for a bit," said Dug.

"Since we left London. The first time," Dig confirmed.

Ditch agreed with a nod.

"The first time… how many times have you left London? When did you leave London?"

Dug lifted Ditch's flat cap from his head and pulled out a yellowed piece of paper, which he handed to Dig, who handed it to me saying, "We've spent a lot of time around you folks, and got to know your ways, but we never got very good with letters. We know the numbers but only in Latin."

"Careful, we don't do Latin around here," I said and unfolded the brittle slip of paper. It was the front page of 'The Times' newspaper. The date read, 2 October 1882. I refolded it and handed it back to Dug who replaced it under Ditch's hat on Ditch's nodding head.

"I don't know how to tell you this," I said, "but you've been digging for over a hundred years."

"A hundred years!" Dug wheezed.

"A hundred years!" Dig shouted triumphantly, "I told you so, I win! Not as long as you thought ah Ditch. What did I tell ya, I win the bet, that's brilliant. Thanks Bottle, nice one, you just won me my bet. My turn to ride now," he kicked his drum across the floor to his brother and then put his hand in his mouth and let out a high-pitched whistle.

Out of the darkness came the scurry of tiny feet, as into the dim light came a phalanx of tiny black moles, each tied by their fat waists by a thin silken thread to a battered old passenger train door. Dig rubbed his hands together with glee, jumped onto the door and sprawled out on it; and instantly fell asleep.

"Sorry about that," said Dug, "but he has been walking for the last twenty years or so. We take it in turns you see, helps us keep up the pace, we can't stand being late. Better late than never; better never late, that's what we say, right Ditch?"

Ditch nodded.

At that very moment, in a rush of panic, I remembered exactly what I was meant to be doing and where I was meant to be, "I need to get home. I need to see my Mum. I need to find a way out of here."

"Out?" Dug said looking at me in disbelief, "why'd you want to do that?"

"I need to get back to Avalon so I can go home, I'm meant to be meeting up with my dad…" I said, almost shouting, "I have no idea what time it is, I'm probably late, I need to get home," and headed off into the darkness.

"Hold on!" Dug shouted, "just hold on, we're coming with you."

"Why?" I shouted back without stopping.

The tiny drum banged behind me and the sound of a thousand scurrying feet followed, to which was added the sound of Dig's low rumbling snore.

"The thing is," Dug huffed, as he jogged beside me, "I reckon you must have an idea where you're going?"

I stopped and stared down at him, giving him my best attempt at furious, "no, not really. I have no idea what I'm doing, but I know I'm not staying down here."

"So you know where you want to go?" his little voice pleaded.

"Yes."

"And you've seen it, Avalon, you've seen it."

"Yes."

"Well then…that's very nearly a plan. So we'll stick with you."

Dug struck up a beat on the little drum and marched off past me into the darkness, followed by the nodding Ditch and finally the snoring Dig on his mole powered sled. For a moment I considered running away in the other direction but the thought of being lost and alone in that darkness was too horrible; so I hurried along after them.

Before then I don't think I'd ever seen a mole up close. They were bigger than I thought, about the size of my hand. It was their plump, muscular shape that was really impressive, they were like black velvet tubes of solid muscle that scurried along at an incredible pace, and they even seemed to enjoy pulling the sled.

"How do you get them to do that?" I asked.

Ditch heard my question, winked and pointed to a rusty tin tied around his waist. He opened it to reveal a mass of squirming bright yellow worms.

"Graveyard worms," Dug called back.

Ditch nodded and offered me one.

"No thanks."

Ditch threw the worm down in front of us and the moles rushed forward pulling the cart after them – obviously, graveyard worms are very, very good worms.

"So how did you meet the Apple Man?" Dug asked over his shoulder.

"How? I'm not sure I can remember, something to do with an orchard, or going to see an orchard, or was that later? My memory today is really weird." I really couldn't recall.

"Tea break!" Dug shouted at the top of his voice, "tea break!"

The two brothers rushed around and before I could take another step forward, they were sitting on the floor with a small kettle boiling away on a little camp stove.

"Right let's hear the story then," said Dug, warming his hands on the tiny fire.

"I don't really remember very much. I think I was with the Apple Man. He was carrying me. I fell off and met this hare and some arguing trees. I tried to help out… but then… it's all very muddy."

"Princesses! Where's the princesses in this story? There's always princesses," Dug bellowed.

"Yes there was a princess, or perhaps she was a queen. She had long hair, very red hair long read hair…"

"Sulis," the brothers pronounced, "and most definitely a queen."

"She was very lovely but," the memory drifted back, "I think she tried to kill me."

Dug sighed and shook his head, "She's not been right since the Romans took her spring and tried to change her name…but she was lovely in her day," Dug said with a grin, "try not to take it to heart Bottle."

"And then…" I tried to recall, "something grabbed me and the next thing I know I'm here."

"Something, what sort of something?" he asked nervously.

"I didn't see it, it wound round my waist and pulled me here, yes that's right, it grabbed me and pulled me here…"

The two brothers burst into peals of laughter and much tea was spat and spilt, "Same thing happened to Ditch years and years ago…let's see, we was digging tin down in Cornwall. There was a King called Henry on the throne. Well, we was doing what we does best and trying to help out the human miners, who really aren't half as good as they thinks they are, I mean using children and all. Well, some of the buggers set a trap for us, and blow me up, they caught Ditch! They called him a devil and decided to burn him! How we laughed! They tied him to a pole in a market square, up top that is, not underground but up top; nasty place. They piled wood round him and set it on fire! Next thing he knows he's being dragged back underground and thrown into an old mine shaft. Took us five years to find him…what larks…never been the same since really. He's much chattier now."

Ditch nodded.

"So what was it?"

"I don't rightly know, but I'll tell you this, Avalon looks after its own," Dug emptied his cup and handed it back to Ditch, "better get going then…"

"You don't know…is that it? You don't know?"

"Yes, that be it."

"Don't you want to know?

"No…I'll leave that to you Bottle. I can see you are very good at wanting to know. We do tunnels. Each to his own Bottle, each to his own."

"He's right." Dig snorted, "I mean look at this tunnel, it's a beauty."

"You dug this tunnel?"

"Who else do you fink done it, rabbits? Course we did," Dig yawned, "we dug it the first time we left London didn't we."

"It's a good tunnel," Dug said proudly. Ditch confirmed this with two firm nods.

"In that casr, you know where this tunnel goes…where does it go?"

"Somewhere between, London, York and here, and has done ever since we dug it."

I had to think about that statement, "so you dug this tunnel a hundred years ago. And you've been going around and around in it ever since, for a hundred years."

Dug put his hands on his hips and gave me a firm look, "it's a mighty big tunnel and tunnels need checking and maintenance young Bottle! Safety first!"

"Yes of course…but you've been going in a circle for a hundred years. Going in a circle and never finding Avalon, because you've kept going in the same circle."

Ditch nodded and Dug agreed.

"So, now you know we're under Avalon, all you have to do is, what?" I looked at them hoping for a spark of understanding, it wasn't there, "what if you dig up?"

Dug turned white with shock and Ditch fell flat on his face in a dead faint.

"Up! We don't do up! We is tunnelling folk, we do down and across, round and about, not up! Never up!"

"But I need to go up, to get out."

"You dig it then! Up indeed! As if, what kind of Knocker do you take me for?!"

"Okay then, just change direction! These are the Hollow Hills aren't they? You people used to live here underground! We're bound to find someone or something, a ladder maybe, a staircase, a way out! But if we keep going round and round where you've already been… well you'll never find anybody not ever."

Dug rubbed his hat into his head, "but that would mean digging new tunnels."

"Yes, it would, but you're good at that right?"

"Hug a mole! Let's do it! Ditch! Dig!" he shouted, "get up, we've a tunnel to dig."

Ditch and Dig jumped to their feet, grabbed each other by the back of their necks, counted to three and then smashed their heads together. But instead of crumbling to the floor, their heads lit up, bathing the whole tunnel in a pale green light.

"What was that?" I exclaimed.

"Headlights of course," Dug pronounced, "safety first."

"Which way is it to be?" said Dig.

"As this is Bottle's tunnel, Bottle decides, which way is it to be?"

I looked at the muddy walls, "That way," and pointed to my left.

Dug stood before the muddy wall, turned the drum to his back and produced a large, wooden handled flint axe from inside his jacket. Using its edge he drew a large five-pointed star across the wall. Then holding the axe high above his head with feet firmly set apart, he said in the calmest and strongest voice you can imagine, "Ditch... unleash the moles."

There was a wild squealing and then the suddenly freed moles charged the pentangle. Mud flew in every direction, great clods of earth bouncing off walls, with Ditch and Dig running around like berserker goal keepers, catching the debris in mid-air and pushing into the tunnel's walls – thereby keeping the path of the sled clear – and all this happened at an incredible speed. In minutes they'd shifted six feet of earth, which is a lot – that's not just six feet in length; you've got to add width, height and depth too - perhaps not so much height as they were short men - but that's still a lot of digging! And then, without warning, the moles stopped digging and ran beside the sled for cover, "what's going on 'ere then?" Dug rasped.

Ditch stepped forward, pressed a muddy finger to his lips, bid us be quiet, and put his shining green head against the newly revealed face of the tunnel. Licking his finger, he marked out the shape of a large uneven rectangle hidden beneath the mud, a shape I wouldn't have seen if I'd stared at it for a month.

"It's a wall," Dig whispered.

"Now what's that doing there?" Dug frowned.

"Walls don't grow themselves," Dig observed.

Ditch and Dig put their shoulders to the marked stone and pushed. It fell forward into deep darkness, and the crashing echo of its fall resounded on and on, like a repeated gun salute.

"Sounds big," Dug whispered, "there's a lot of space in there. Are you ready for this Bottle?"

I nodded, and one by one, we climbed through the hole. Once inside the bother's headlights reveled a tiny portion of a seemingly endless stone lined hall. There was only one thing to say, and I said it, "wow."

WOWwowowowwow throbbed back at me like a giant's hiccup. And for an instant, I searched the room just to check a giant wasn't in there with us. It was exactly the kind of place a giant should be...and this was Avalon after all.

As soon as I stepped forward something wet touched my face; and I made exactly the kind of sound you wouldn't want to make in a giant's hall - a half yelp, half scream. The hall quaked with the sound. If there was a giant in there, it now knew I was there too. Dug gave me a look, and Ditch nearly fell over choking in silent laughter. The wet thing that had made me jump was a bundle of long-tangled roots that had squeezed through the stone roof. Masses of it hung around us like long wet stringy hair.

Slowly and as quietly as we could we advanced into the room, I pushed a loom of roots aside and was immediately drenched in a shower of cold water that left my teeth chattering.

"Shhhh," Dug insisted sharply.

The green light from the brothers' heads began to fade to a very unpleasant and spooky shade of green which really didn't improve the situation at all. Everything about the room was telling me, 'You shouldn't be here,' but on we went. Side stepping the tangled trestles of roots as best we could, we made our way deeper into the vast hall.

Dug pointed at something white and glowing, hidden within the curtain of roots, and stated flatly, "We shouldn't be here."

His confirmation of my feelings was disturbing, "Why? What is it? What do you see?"

"Too many questions Bottle, only one answer, We need to go," he insisted nervously.

Ditch took hold of my arm and tried to pull me back towards the hole in the wall. I pulled my arm free and although my teeth were now knocking together because I was scared and not just cold and wet, I made my way towards the curtain of wet roots; took a deep breath and stepped through.

Five giant stone warriors loomed above me. Armour clad, shields on their backs, they leant on huge drawn swords, with their bowed stone heads and shoulders shrouded in a cascade of roots. At the centre of their circle, was a long white stone table on which laid another knight, a large man but no giant, as pale and still as the stone he was laid upon.

"Who is it? Is he dead?"

"Not enough I wouldn't wonder, and we don't want to wake him. We need to go," Dug whispered, sounding more frantic with every word.

"But who is it?"

"Humans and their questions…who is it indeed?" he mumbled, "look at his robes boy." The man was wrapped in a thick red cloak from head to toe although the grey metal chainmail around his neck and head was still visible, and the thick beard and hair that lay outside of the chainmail would have been as white as the marble table, if it wasn't flecked with dark red stains which I just knew had to be blood.

"He looks like a king."

"A king, you say. He's a king alright, but I'll not speak his name here. It could break the charm." I tried to take another step forward but Dug gripped my arm and pulled me back. "No Bottle. We do not want to wake him. The day Avalon needs him again, will be a sorry day for us all, leave him be."

I tried leaning in to get a closer look but Dug yanked me back by several steps and then pulled me down until I was face to face with him.

"We have to go," I could tell by the look on his face that he was very scared indeed. "Listen to me Bottle, this is no Henry, George or Victoria this is a real king! A blood and sword king! A warrior, a slaughterer, a baby killer…we have to go."

The huge room suddenly seemed very cold. I looked at the still pale face and saw what Dug saw there. Yes, that was the face of a man who had done terrible things to get what he wanted, even in his sleep the lines on his face were deep and hard, and I knew that even his dreams were dark.

We quickly retraced our steps and headed back to the hole we'd made. Ditch was already through and hurriedly beckoned us on. Now that we were leaving, I couldn't wait to get out, both Dug and I looked over our shoulders waiting for the icy unseen hand that was going to grab us and stop our exit and even when we were through the wall we all peered back into the dark hall to make sure nobody was following.

"We have to reseal it. We have to reseal it right now!" Dug said, his voice full of panic.

"We'll never lift that stone."

Dug rubbed his head and walked in circles thinking aloud, "Perhaps…we could undermine the foundation and make this section collapse."

"How long will that take?" I asked.

"Hard to tell, a day or two maybe."

"No, I need to see my Mum," I said more loudly than I intended, "think of something else. There's got to be another way. My Dad is going to kill me."

"Are they allowed to do that these days? My, my how things have changed…"

Dig coughed, rubbed his nose and said in an exceptionally low rumbling voice, "would that be an apple orchard?"

"What are you talking about? I need to get home," I insisted.

"You were with the Apple Man, before you got lost," he replied slowly and thoughtfully, as if the idea had not yet fully formed, "and weren't those apple roots?"

Dug took a deep breath and leant back into the hall's darkness, "yep, them is apple roots alright."

"Must be apple trees up there then, stands to reason," Dig added, "apple roots means apple trees."

"We're under the orchard, the Apple Man might still be there."

"Reckon so," said Dug.

Ditch nodded.

"So how do I get up there?" I asked, standing up straight and banging my head on the roof of the tunnel.

"Don't rightly know," said Dig.

"Well couldn't you dig up there!" I pleaded.

"I don't like up, but on this occasion. I thinks the quicker we part company, the better for us all I reckon," said Dug wiping his brow with his sleeve.

"What does that mean?" I blurted, feeling hurt by his comment.

"I'll tell you what it means. We've been tunnelling for hundreds and hundreds of years, and we never ran into no kings before. One trip with you, and its cursed kings all over the place, and the Pendragon no less. So yes, I blames you and I thinks it's best we go our separate ways."

"That's not fair!" I shouted and was instantly shushed by all three brothers.

"I don't know about no fair or otherwise. We'll keep on digging our way and you young Bottle," he looked me up and down scornfully, "you need to get out."

"And I want to get out, that's all I wanted, I want to go home."

"Right then," Dig scratched his nose and nodded, "up it is then. You two backfill and close-up this hole. Me and Bottle will climb up and over. I'll meet you back here and then we go back to our tunnel and no messing," Dig said firmly.

Dug and Ditch nodded.

Dig drew a long flint knife from his jacket, strode up to the exposed stone wall, and bashed his head against it, reigniting he's head's green glow; "Off we go then," he declared and began clambering up the wall. Moments later he'd disappeared up to his waist in the mud above us.

Dug shrugged sulkily, "better get going then, before something else happens."

"I will, I'm going…" I said, just as sulkily, and then I remembered their kindness to me, "thank you for the clothes, and the shoes. I'm sorry if I've caused you trouble."

Dug shrugged – but a little less sulkily.

Ditch smiled a big cheesy grin, knelt before me and with a gentle nod directed me to place my foot in his cupped hands. I did as I was bid and with one swift lift, I was clambering into the hole his brother's feet had just disappeared into.

Chapter 17

Dig's tunnel was only just big enough to crawl through on my hands and knees. Even Dig was crawling, but the space he'd cleared with his flashing knife gave his shoulders plenty of space but mine being slightly broader, were pressed tightly against each wall. I had to keep my chin pressed into my chest to stop my head grating against the low roof. My hands and knees were having the worst of it, one moment they were squashing soft mud, and the next they were striking against hard stone.

Dig's method of digging was impressive, it was a wild spinning motion that left me dizzy and covered with mud. In a few short minutes my neck was aching, my hands were too sore to lean on and my knees were rubbed raw.

"How much further?" I shouted as loudly as I could with my chin in my chest, which couldn't have been loud enough, because Dig just kept going, his feet disappeared into the darkness. Trying to keep up was useless and soon even the sound of his digging faded to nothing, and I found myself alone in the dark.

I lay on my belly and wriggled up the tunnel as best I could. Occasionally lifting my head and shouting for help, I made slow painful progress, until a huge lump of mud dislodged and fell directly in my path. I tried to push past it, but my back scrapped along the roof of the tunnel, and I felt it budge, heard a deep wet slurp, and felt the tunnel collapse around me.

The next thing I remember, I was waking up spitting mud with the Apple Man throwing apple cores at my head.

"There we go! Right as rain!" he grinned.

"What happened?" I coughed.

"The Knocker dragged you up and left."

"He did? What happened to you? You left me, you promised to get me home and you left me!"

"You stopped before I did."

"I fell off."

"It is much the same thing in the end."

"No, it is not! It is not the same thing at all! And you said you'd get me home, you promised. I have to get home! What time is it now?"

The Apple Man looked at the sun and then at the shadows on the floor, "it's a shadow past the middle of the day."

"What does that mean?" I shouted.

"Time enough to see the trees," the Apple Man said with glee, as he took hold of my hand and pulled me to my feet, "it is good to see you again Bottle, are we still friends?"

I looked at the raggedy green skinned old man and couldn't think why I should be his friend, but I knew I was, "I guess so. Yes, we are friends Apple Man."

"Good, that is good. So, let me welcome you friend Bottle, to the Isle of Apples, the sacred heart of Avalon, my orchard."

We were standing within a circle of twelve trees, and around them I could see another larger circle and perhaps there was another circle beyond that, I really couldn't say, I was too taken up by the way each tree was linked to the next. The side branches of each tree touched and wrapped round its neighbour, forming a huge unbroken circle, but the most incredible thing was that each tree, although bare of leaves, as they should have been in early spring, carried one perfect apple.

"The trees have saved the last apple for me," the Apple Man said, "it is a mark of kindness and respect. Alas, I have checked each one carefully but …she is not here," he said with a sigh.

"She? You mean another Wodwo. I'm sorry Apple Man, but you're not really alone, you've got lots of people… well things, that care about you, the Crone, Thorn… me."

He nodded sadly, reached out a long spindly arm and pulled an apple from a tree and held it out to me. One half was the most vivid green and the other was as red as blood. It was perfectly shaped, glowing with health, a truly perfect apple.

"Taste it, you'll never taste better."

"Thank you but no. I've been told what happens if I eat here," I replied, putting my hands into my pockets.

"Ah yes, time changes for those that are Avalon, they are blessed with good health, and long life. Doctor Apple keeps the day away, as the old saying goes," he said, placing the apple gently on the grass beside me, "but the apple is yours, my gift to you, just in case you change your mind." He lolloped over to another tree and twisted another lone apple from its branch. This one he sniffed, shook, rolled in-between his hands and then savagely bit into, taking half the apple in one bite. He crunched loudly, very loudly, then fell on his back and started rocking from side to side, with juice oozing out of the corners of his mouth exclaiming, "Oh joy! Taste the sweet sunshine the fine rain, oh the coolness of the night!"

"Oh come on, it's just an apple," I moaned. "isn't it a bit like cannibalism for you…I mean, you're eating your family."

"No Bottle. I am eating the fruit my family have made for me… doesn't food always taste better when someone else has made it? Wait, I have a thought… I have a job for you."

"Oh yes what's that?" I had grown very suspicious of these 'Good Folk Jobs,' "are you wanting some shopping done, if that's the case, forget it."

"Apple crumble. What's the recipe? How do you make it?"

"I don't know…apples and crumble I guess."

"And the yellow gold that drapes over it," he said with tears in his eyes.

"Yellow gold?" I had to think, "do you mean custard?"

"Yes! Custardy custard made by Birds they said; but which kind I could never fathom, canaries perhaps," he said with a tap, tap to his nose.

"No Apple Man that's not right, it's not birds…" How to explain? "I'll get you the recipe or make some or..." and I heard myself say it, "buy you some on my next shopping trip."

"You will!" he shouted. "Look, take these, take these!" saying this he began running around the trees picking apples, "crumbly crumble was always good! But imagine how good it will be when made with the last apples from Avalon. What a joy, a worthy gift for the Beltane feast!" He shuddered to a stop and handed me an armful of apples.

"I can't carry all these."

"But you must, you must, please, please! For the Beltane feast and the custardy custard and the joy! Oh the joy of the crumbly crumble!"

It was like listening to a four year old, "I can't carry these home!" I insisted, "and I do need to get home. I have to get home. I'm tired Apple Man, tired and very dirty. I need to get home."

"Very well then, let us bargain. Say you'll make me a crumbly crumble," he held an apple core in front of my face, "and you'll be out of Avalon before this fruit hits the ground?"

I looked him in the eye, "is this a trick? You're going to stick it on a branch or something …"

"No, this is no trick, a fair bargain" his eyes sparkled, "do we have a bargain?"

I had my doubts, but it was worth a try, "Oh alright then, before it hits the ground."

"Quickly take off that garment," he said pointing at the ancient mud-stained jacket. I did as he asked and handed him the jacket. He piled the apples into it and handed me the bundle. Then stepping back, he swung his arm around and around, until it whistled and whizzed and then with a shout of "Up!" He launched the apple core high into the sky. It went straight up and disappeared from sight.

I jumped onto the Apple Man's back and we were off and running; "a Yew tree Bottle, we need a Yew Tree!" he yelled, as he raced forward.

We'd cleared the orchard and were now running around it at an alarming speed. On our right was the orchard, on our left a wood but both were just a blur. I tried to spot a Yew tree but at that speed, I could hardly tell one tree from another let alone their species.

"Yewtreeyewtreeyewtreeyewtreeyewtree," the Apple Man garbled, getting quicker with every stride, "it's falling! Oh the crumble! Yewtreeyewtreeyew…"

"Stop!" I shouted and pointed. There it was; a huge twisted Yew tree, at least four feet across at its base, its dark spiky leaves rich and glossy, shining out against the dullness of the bare leafless trees surrounding it.

Three strides later and the Apple man had carried me to it. There was a huge gaping hole at the centre of the Yew, as its middle was dead and rotted away. I couldn't see how this old tree was going to help. I jumped from his arms, holding the bundle of apples tight to my chest. I looked behind us, in the distance I could see the falling apple core, sparkling like a ball of falling ice.

"See you soon Bottle!" the Apple Man shouted grabbing me by the arm and shoving me inside the Yew. "Oh Yew Tree, oh Yew tree," he spoke very quickly, "take my friend to his land out of our land through your land to a nearby land but not to his final resting place…oh tree of death!"

"What!?" I shouted.

Chapter 18

I don't know if the Apple Man heard my shout, I'm not even sure I heard it, things moved that quickly.

One moment I was shouting in Avalon, the next I was stepping out of the Yew tree into an overgrown graveyard on the edge of the estate, not far from the superstore. He'd done it, somehow, he'd done it; the Apple Man had kept his promise and got me home…well almost, close enough anyhow.

It would have been nice to be able to get back through the estate without being seen but it wasn't going to happen. I was covered with mud, and my ancient trousers didn't know whether to cling to me or fall off in tatters. I looked a right state, and everybody I passed thought they had the right to express the same opinion. If there is one thing that's sure to make you feel wetter, colder and muddier, its people pointing out how wet, cold and muddy you look!

I decided to get off the main street and took a short cut through a back alley; it cut the journey down but did mean dodging round spilt rubbish and dog dirt, but let's face it I wasn't going to get any dirtier. I was just passing a half-melted fire scorched green bin when I heard someone behind me. I spun around but there was no one there, I turned back and there was Thorn.

"What have you got there Bottle?"

I held the sodden bundle of apples tight to my chest, "Apples from the Apple Man's orchard, he gave them to me."

"Is that so?"

"He wants me to make him something. What are you doing here?"

He took a step towards me and before I could raise an eyebrow; I was on my back with Thorn's flint knife under my chin.

"I know your heart Bottle. Be warned, that which belongs to Avalon, stays in Avalon."

"The Apple Man gave them to me! He gave them to me."

"That is as it may be, but you will have to live with the choices you make little one… you have been warned."

The flint blade pressed into my chin, his eyes glinted and then he was gone. I was lying on my back in a dirty alley staring up at the sky and I just knew I'd landed in a big pile of dog dirt.

I got home to find a note from Dad, saying he'd be back in an hour. I threw the dirty clothes out into the garden, hid the Avalon apples under my bed, and jumped in the shower. Where I scrubbed for all I was worth, but as I washed off the layers of mud, I couldn't help hearing the Apple Man's words about, 'Doctor Apple,' wrapped around Thorn's warning; and an idea began to form itself around the desperate hope that I could save my mum. I put on clean clothes and made my way as quickly as I could to the hospice with an Avalon apple in my pocket. I couldn't have been more aware of it had it been a bar of gold.

Dad was sitting beside Mum's bed when I arrived, he shushed me with a raised finger and we stepped out of the room into the corridor.

"Sorry son, I was coming to get you, but I lost track of time."

"You're not the only one. How's Mum?"

"Asleep, she didn't have such a goodnight but she's comfortable now."

"Has she eaten?"

"Had some fruit juice for breakfast."

The Avalon apple felt as hot as a coal in my pocket. Mum was lying on her side facing the door as we walked in. Her eyes fluttered open briefly at the sound of our voices, a slight smile crossed her face and then vanished. As quietly as we could, Dad and I pulled up a couple of blue plastic chairs and sat together watching Mum as she slept. I think both of us were trying to burn the picture of her sleeping into our skulls. It was a very easy way to spend some time but before long my stomach started to rumble in protest.

"Did you get your room sorted?" Dad asked.

I nodded and yawned and then my stomach groaned some more.

Dad looked at his watch, "Have you eaten?"

I shook my head and yawned again.

Dad handed me a five-pound note, "Go to the canteen, get something hot to eat and then get yourself off home."

"I want to stay," I emphasised my commitment with another yawn.

"You're falling asleep Kay, go on," his words were swallowed up by a huge yawn.

I pointed at his yawn and then added another of my own.

"Okay, okay…chip shop and bed it is then," Dad laughed. He stood and leant over Mum and kissed her head and she snuggled down under the covers. I kissed her too, but all I could smell was the hospital – she didn't smell like Mum anymore, that rotten horrible sickness had changed her smell; I was losing her; I couldn't let that happen. I took the apple out of my pocket and placed it on the bedside locker.

"Nice looking apple. But I'm not sure she's up to crunching her way through that."

"I got it for Mum. It will do her good, make her feel better. The Apple doctor keeps the day away."

Dad smiled, "I'm not sure that's right, but…" He took a pen out of his pocket and a piece of paper from another and handed them to me. I wrote, "For Mum, from Kay. Hands off."

Chapter 19

We took the chips home that night and ate them in front of the TV. It was some stupid film about cavemen and dinosaurs. The main point of the film was the female star who ran around in a fur bikini who fell in love with a hairy man from a different tribe and that was about it; pretty dumb. The bit I do remember, was when the hairy hero – who falls for the girl in the fur bikini – was hiding in an apple tree while these nasty brutal monkey men fought over the fallen apples and ended up killing each other. I wondered if the Good Folk had been around when the dinosaurs were about or if they came later? I wondered how the Apple Man would deal with a T-Rex and what he'd think about monkey men eating his apples? I can't remember how the film ended, so either I fell asleep or it's a really bad film…or perhaps it's a really bad film which is why I fell asleep. That night my dreams were full of apples and dinosaurs, Good Folk and being buried alive. It was a relief to wake up.

Dad was long gone by the time I came downstairs and I was glad of it. I was so sore I couldn't have kept pace with the milk float even if I'd wanted to, and anyway I had a promise to keep and apple crumble to make.

I'm certainly no cook now, and I certainly wasn't then, what made me think I could make a decent crumble mystifies me to this day; but you don't know what you don't know, so I gave it a go. I found Mum's favourite cookbook, which told you how to cook a hundred things you've never even heard of and even more you'd never want to eat, but it did have a big section on puddings with step-by-step instructions. These included five different types of 'perfect crumble.' I got busy and set to work. I washed and pealed the apples, cut them into slices and put the slices in a bowl of water so they didn't brown; that bit was pretty easy, and I did it without losing a finger. The next stage was the crumble. The instructions were, work together flour, sugar and butter – that's crumble – flour, sugar and butter. Did we have any flour in the house? No, we did not.

The only money I had was the Good Folk's money. I was baking for them so why not use it? The Apple Man had kept his promise and now I had to keep mine. I stuffed the money into my jeans and headed for the superstore.

Don't you think it's odd how much we talk about weather but never really remember it? People have very short memories when it comes to the weather and I'm sure I'm no better, but I seem to remember that morning as bright and warm. Spring was finally winning through, and the world was cheering up. Even the people at the entrance to the superstore were smiling at each other and of course they were talking about the weather. I kept my head down, grabbed a trolley and hurried in. A quick glance about told me my least favourite security guard was nowhere around, which made the day seem even brighter. I found the 'home baking' aisle and looked for flour. Only to discover that flour isn't just flour, oh no, there's plain, self-raising, strong, malt and whole meal, to name a few. The recipe said plain, so I got the biggest I could find, and was putting it in the trolley when my arm was grabbed by the smirking bulk of my least favourite security guard.

"No Easter eggs today then?" he said.

"Not today thanks," I said pulling my arm free, only to find my way was blocked by a large, uniformed police officer.

"You're coming with us son."

Chapter 20

The next thing I knew, I was sitting at a table in the stores back office with two very large policemen standing over me. They were friendly enough, one of them; he had short red hair, even gave me a can of pop, but they were still very big policemen, and I was very scared.

A short lady, wearing huge round glasses beneath a harsh black fringe; she looked as if she were wearing an oversized helmet; walked into the room, followed by a serious looking man in a tight dark suit, and an even darker frown. As soon as the policemen saw him, they stepped out of the room. The lady sat next to me and opened a large plastic file.

"Hello, is it Kay? My name's Elaine, I'm a social worker and it's my job to make sure you're safe and that no one frightens you. I'm here because your father isn't here at the minute…"

"Where is he?"

"He's safe. The police are interviewing him at present, and they want to ask you some questions… is that all right? Are you happy to answer a few questions?"

"Is my Dad all right? Why are the police talking to him? What's happened?"

The man in the dark suit joined us at the table. Elaine paused, and waited for the man to introduce himself, he didn't. He remained silent and fixed his concentrated frown upon me, I immediately felt guilty – but I didn't know why.

"Kay, this is Detective Inspector Sims, and he'd like you to answer some questions. But before you do that I want you to know, you're not in trouble, the police just need you to answer some questions for them," she turned to the frowning Sims and calmly stated, "Kay wants to know that his Dad is all right."

Sims nodded and then looked me straight in the eye. I had the feeling that his friendliest look was equal to my dad's most serious stare. This was not a man you lied to, he'd know you were lying, and then there would be trouble.

"Your dad's fine. He's down at the station helping us with a problem we've got to straighten out," he spoke with a voice that sounded like moving gravel, as he pulled a packet of cigarettes from his pocket. Elaine scowled at him and coughed. He replaced the packet with an air of annoyance, "as soon as it's straightened out, we'll get him up here to get you," Elaine scowled and coughed again, but this time Sims scowled back, and Elaine withered into her chair, "now I'm hoping you can help us too, would you do that Kay? Are you willing to help?"

A nod was all I could manage.

"Great," Sims said, pulling a roll of money from his jacket pocket. He laid a note down in front of me. It was a twenty-pound note, "this is a note you used to pay for some shopping here earlier this week. Can you tell me where you got it?"

"I found it," as soon as I said it, I knew it was the wrong thing to say. Sims didn't believe me and why should he, my dad hadn't believed me either. I didn't believe me, "A lady gave it to me," I blurted out.

"Really… and why did she do that?"

"It was a reward."

"A twenty quid reward, you must have done something great to earn a twenty quid reward; what was it?"

I decided to stick to the same story Dad had believed, and told them how we'd found the old farmer, and how I'd returned to the house and been rewarded by his family – none of which was exactly true, but most of which was accurate. But I could feel my body wasn't going to let me hide the fact that I knew I was in the wrong. I felt hot and sweaty, and I must have been as red as a pillar box.

"Is that so?" Sims' frown darkened, "so how much did they give you Kay? Do you remember? Was it this much?" he put another twenty-pound note in front of me, "or was it this much?" he put another down, "maybe this much?" he slapped down another three, "or…" he pulled another wedge of money from his pockets, and waved them under my nose, "maybe this much. That's a very big thank you isn't it Kay?"

"It's true," I lied again, "it was given to me," I insisted – which was true.

"I almost believe you, perhaps someone did give you this money to spend but…" Sims whispered, "the trouble is…see this number?" he pointed to the bill's identification number, "I'm sure you know this, but each note has its own number. No two numbers on any bill are ever the same. But what we have here is eight bills with the same number. The ten-pound notes are just the same, identical numbers… and you know what that means don't you?"

Yes, I did. It meant that the Good Folk had got hold of two notes, a twenty and a ten, and they'd made lots and lots of identical copies: absolutely identical copies. Whether by magic or skill the Good Folk had been forging money, "they're forgeries," I heard myself say.

"Very good… that's right and that's a very, very serious crime isn't it Kay?" Sims scowled.

And of course, the police thought I was mixed up in it and what's more; I was! Even though I hadn't known it! But then it hit me; the police thought that both dad and I were mixed up in it! And I had got Dad mixed up it in – this was my fault! We were in serious, serious trouble.

"So, I'm going to ask you again, where did you get this money?"

I was ready to tell him the truth. I was going to tell him about the fairies and the Apple Man, about a talking walking stick called Fiddle, and a nettle bush called Nettle. How Hill wreaked Stonehenge, and how the mighty Haggis built a bridge. I was going to come clean about everything but as soon as I opened my mouth, I stopped. How on earth could I expect a policeman to believe me? He wouldn't, of course he wouldn't, but if I did tell him what I knew, what would he do? He'd send officers round to check the farm. Perhaps they already had? They'd find Avalon, and what would happen to Avalon then? What would happen to me? My contract would be well and truly broken and if that happened, I'd soon find myself roasting over the fire or chopped and boiling in the cauldron! But what else could I do? I had to tell them.

Chapter 21

I heard a tapping sound behind me. We all turned to see a very tall thin man dressed in a long grey tailcoat, standing with his back to us, tapping his walking stick against the floor.

"Oi you!" Sims snapped, "what you playing at? How'd you get in here?"

Without a glance in our direction the man shrugged, sniffed and threw a small hessian sack high over his shoulder; it landed at the centre of the table with a thud, making Elaine jump.

"Oi, you!" Sims shouted, "get out! Officers," he yelled at the door, and the two policemen who'd been waiting outside rushed in.

"How did he get in here?" said the redheaded officer.

"You tell me, you were on the door! Get him out of here," Sims shouted, "right you out! Now!"

The man turned to face us. He had an enormous, pointed nose, under which he sported a curling waxed moustache that was wider than his head. He had a monocle in his left eye, whilst his right seemed to be made from white marble, but it was his nose that caught your attention it was so long and pointed he could have spiked olives from a jar with it, if he'd wanted to.

"Didn't you hear me ..." Sims choked, staring at the man's visage in disbelief, "good grief … I told you to get out. Is that a mask?"

"Shut up human," the walking stick said with a sneer as it sprung its arms and legs.

"Eek," said Elaine.

"Got your attention have we? Good," Fiddle laughed.

The room was in total silence, and I was the only one smiling.

Fiddle pranced over to the hessian sack and reached inside it, "And now for our next trick, I would ask you to observe. No mirrors, no strings, no tricks, just one Boggit." He held aloft a lumpy, bumpy and very knobbly, moss coloured little man.

"Hello, Bottle," said Bog with a wave, "sorry about the drowning thing, Sulis sends her love."

I waved back.

"What is this?" Sims's voice quivered.

"I think I'm having a flashback," Elaine the social worker whimpered.

"Then you'll love this," jeered the pointy nosed man, tearing off the mask to reveal Thorn's pale angular face. Elaine nearly fell off her chair.

Fiddle placed Bog onto the table, and then using his spindly legs as drumsticks, began tapping out a rhythm to which the sneering Thorn added a hum; Bog started to dance.

It was a knobbly dance, a crooked and twisted dance but it had rhythm and a bounce all of its own, you just couldn't look away. Sims, Elaine and the two policemen all gathered around the table to watch. Thorn was suddenly behind me. He grabbed me by the throat with one hand and with the other he covered my nose and mouth, I couldn't breathe. I thought he was going to kill me right there in front of the police?

There is no nice way to describe what happened next. Bog wriggled, cranked and strained, bent over double and let out the loudest, longest fart I've ever heard. The air turned green and so did all those gathered about; the humans that is.

"There's an old saying," Fiddle giggled, "and it says, nought gets done sitting in the sun and nought smells as bad as a Boggit's bum. Can't smell a thing myself of course… but by the look on your faces, I'd say there's some truth in it."

Elaine was the first to pass out, followed by the red-haired policeman, then his friend and finally Sims crashed to the floor.

"Get to it," Thorn barked out, squeezing my nose a little tighter, "quickly, Bottle's turning blue, aren't you bluebottle."

"Humans," Fiddle giggled, "nicely done Bog."

"It's a gift," Bog replied humbly.

Fiddle shook the sack out of the table and ten bright blue frogs dropped out at Bog's feet, "Looks like we brought too many"

"Use them all," Thorn ordered as he moved one hand under my chin and lifted me out of the chair, "I want them to forget today forever. Bog, can you get yourself home?"

"I'm sure I'll manage, there's sure to be a drain somewhere. Off you go, nice to see you again Bottle, Sulis sends her best," Bog replied, as he dropped a blue frog into Sims' mouth,

Keeping a tight hold of me with one hand, Thorn replaced his mask with the other and then carried me out the door. Once Fiddle had closed the door behind us, Thorn dropped me to the floor. I landed like a crumpled can – guess what, fresh bruises on my bum.

"Lead the way Fiddle," Thorn ordered, and they moved off down the corridor, they didn't even wait for me to catch my breath.

"Wait," I wheezed.

Thorn marched back, grabbed me by the ear and yanked me to my feet, "please feel free to participate in your own rescue Bottle."

"This way!" Fiddle barked, as he opened another door; and there we were back on the busy superstore floor.

It was one of those, 'the whole world stopped' moments. All eyes were on us. Shoppers, young and old mesmerized by the sight of a strange looking man in an ancient tailcoat, yanking a child about by his ear, and then of course there was Fiddle, a walking talking walking stick.

"Boo!" Fiddle shouted, which didn't help the situation.

Three tattooed men with matching beer bellies fell into the wines and spirits, and a lady in a furry pink coat and big hair screamed, ran down the aisle and threw herself into a chest freezer. Alarms rang, bottles smashed, and shelves crashed to the ground, as Thorn grabbed Fiddle, threw me over his shoulder and made for the exit.

"This child is a thief and a ruffian. He will be punished!" he shouted and strode off down the aisle, thwacking me with Fiddle, on every other step, in time with the thwacking. "Make way, make way," Thorn bellowed, "I'll teach you a lesson you'll never forget, mark my words! Flog them it's all they understand!"

"Put me down," I yelled.

"No, put me down!" Fiddle cried, "stop doing that, don't make me touch him, stop it, stop it! That's a human bum! That's disgusting! Stop it!"

Nobody stopped us, nobody came to my rescue, and nobody even said a word, until Edith the cashier stepped into Thorn's path.

"Stop that right now! Put that child down. I said put that child down," Edith's wagging finger was in Thorn's face. "I've never seen anything so disgraceful! Who do you think you are beating a child like that? Put him down at once!"

I had to admire Edith's courage. Thorn stopped and did exactly as he was told. He dropped me. I didn't wait to hear Thorn's reply to Edith's wagging finger. Out the doors I ran, and I didn't look back, I kept going, I needed to get out of there, away from them all. Across the road and back into the estate I went at top speed. I ran till my legs ached and my breathing burnt, and still I didn't stop, until I saw three police cars parked at the end of my street. I hid behind a nearby van and watched six police officers stamping in and out of our house, but the worst of it was the crowd of neighbours and strangers that had gathered to watch the show. My mother would have been mortified. Something hit me on the back of the head. A slice of apple fell at my feet. I turned and saw a nettle bush wave at me. I picked up the apple slice and threw it back at Nettle.

"Thanks Bottle," Nettle said cheerfully holding up a dripping wet sack, "don't worry we got the rest of them out of the house."

"Stuff your apples! What about my dad?"

"He's not in there. The men in blue took him out of the house a long time ago."

"I've got to get him out of there."

"And how do you propose to do that? You couldn't get yourself out of a marketplace unobserved," Thorn hissed through his ridiculous mask.

"What's your game then Bottle? Running off like that, don't you know a rescue when you see one?" said Fiddle giving my ear a sharp tweak, "humans, all as thick as sparrows. What's going on here then?"

"They're searching my house for your dodgy money," I heard myself saying, "and they've got my dad at the police station. We need to find him."

"We? I don't see what this has got to do with us," Fiddle yawned.

"Are you having a laugh? He's there because of the fake money you people made and gave to me."

Thorn shrugged, Fiddle stretched, and nettle chomped down another apple, but a tatty looking bush called Dock stepped forward and said; "it seems to me, that the powers-that-be, have discovered our ruse. I suspect young Bottle here, told his pater he'd found the money at the farm. And that's why they interrogated Bottle, to find the truth of his father's tale…but that doesn't mean the authorities believe Bottle or his father. But in order to find the truth of both their tales…they're going to search the farm."

"A wise weed is Dock," Nettle asserted, "I'd listen to her if I were you."

"Very well, in that case we need to get back," Thorn sighed, "we'll muster a glamour as we did when the old farmer died, it's nothing."

I jumped to my feet and ran at him. Fiddle stepped forward, blocking my path with raised arms, but I just kept going and pushed him aside. I heard something snap. I looked down and one of Fiddle's arms was lying broken under my foot.

"Oh well that's just marvelous isn't it," Fiddle snorted.

"I'm so sorry Fiddle," I said, kneeling, to pick up the broken lifeless twig that had once been his arm.

He snatched it from me and then hit me with it, "I said you should have been called clumsy, did I not!"

"You did. And I'm sorry, can it be fixed?"

"That's not the point but yes it can. I've been glued more times than you've eaten mole soup. The point is… what was the point Thorn?"

Thorn straightened his tailcoat and glared at me, "we cannot help you Bottle, we need to get back. We have to protect ourselves. The glamour worked before; it will work again."

Shaking with rage I walked over to him, grabbed the nose of that stupid mask and yanked it off his face. I stared into those icy lidless eyes, finally impervious to their cold glare.

"You don't know, what you don't know Thorn. Superstores have security cameras; the police aren't going to stop, just because you're let loose some frogs. They've records, paperwork and forms, they're not going to forget forgery. You've committed forgery Thorn, don't any of you know what that means? It's a crime against the crown. A crime against the country. They're going to come for you and they're not going to stop. And I won't let you use my dad as the fall-guy. I will tell them; I'll tell them everything."

Thorn's laugh was cold and hard, "And you'll be a child talking about fairies. Do you expect them to believe you? This world of cameras and forms? I think not."

"I'll do more than that, I'll take them to the farm and take them across Haggis Hop."

"That would be breaking the contract Bottle, and you know what that means don't you?" Thorn hissed.

"I don't care. I'll break the contract every day. A hundred times a day, unless you help my dad!"

Thorn nodded and then smiled. "Very good Bottle… family is everything," he held out his hand to me and smiled again. I was so shocked by the warmth of the smile that I just stared at him, and again he smiled. It was a strange smile. It was honest and jolly and really very friendly, but it just didn't belong on that face. I gave him my hand and he held it softly, "we shall help your father, but they need us now in Avalon. Later when it is dark, we shall free your father. Agreed?"

I wanted Dad saved NOW - but my NOW, was going to have to wait; "swear it," I heard myself say.

"It is so sworn," Thorn declared, "now then Bottle, do you know where we can find a Yew tree?"

Chapter 22

Nettle, Fiddle, Thorn and I stood in the old graveyard before the twisted old Yew. Nettle scuttled round to make sure the place was deserted, which of course it was, and when he was satisfied, he whispered something to the Yew and instantly a deep hollow appeared in its trunk. We all three stepped inside.

"May I?" Fiddle asked.

"Please do," Thorn replied.

Fiddle coughed dryly and began chanting, "Great doorway to our resting place, do not take us too soon to our everlasting place of resting, take us to our home or if you prefer…to our doom."

"What?" I shouted.

By the time the word had left my mouth, we were stepping out of the Yew tree, on Lone Farm's drive.

"Quickly!" Thorn urged as he grabbed my hand and ran for the farmhouse door. I turned my head just in time to see the flashing lights of police cars appearing at the end of the drive.

The door slammed shut behind us. Thorn let go of my hand and pushed open the first door on our right. A crowd of creatures; Leprechauns for sure, each dressed in green jackets and short brown trousers; were busy piling up great stacks of money into huge tottering towers.

"We are discovered!" Thorn barked, "prepare for glamour, destroy it all, it's useless!"

As in one voice the Leprechauns cheered and began stuffing handfuls of money into their mouths.

"They were much happier making shoes," Fiddle sighed as we rushed into the kitchen.

"Prepare to Glamour!" Thorn commanded, "COMMENCE TO GLAMOUR!"

The air was filled with winged beings of all shapes and sizes, some no bigger than dust balls, others big enough to ride insects and yet others as varied in size and shape as the birds of the sky. The air buzzed and heaved with their shimmering dance! They spun around and around, this way and that, until every inch and every corner of the room was filled with them and nothing, but their movement could be seen. They sparkled; they glowed red-hot like flowing lava. The room was consumed by them, the cups and pots, the cauldron and all were swept up, melted into the mass of seething molten heat and then it all just vanished… and then it all came back, and the dirty squalid kitchen was just as dirty and squalid as it was before, nothing had changed. Had the glamour failed?

"What's happened?" a gasped.

Too late, there was a loud bang on the front door, followed by a shout and then the thumping of heavy boots as the police stormed in.

Chapter 23

I stood with my back to the crumbling kitchen wall, Thorn on my left, Nettle on my right with the branch of the tree breaking through the window above my head.

Six police officers marched through the kitchen door, one of them, a stern-faced woman with painted eyebrows and very tight lips, looked right at me and then looked away. She walked into the kitchen, looked out of the window that wasn't there and then turned away.

"She must have seen me!" I thought, I was right in front of her! Thorn put his thin forefinger to my lips, clearly quiet was needed.

The Good Folk were busy being extremely quiet but also extremely naughty. They pulled faces behind the officers' backs; they pulled faces under their very noses. They pretended to kick, bite and scratch. They pretended to shoot arrows at the officers. They held their noses as if smelling a great stink, some of them made a great stink that made the poor officer's eyes water! And still, they didn't see us.

Police sniffer dogs were brought in, and that made me nervous for a moment but I needn't have been, because the Good Folk were soon tickling the dogs behind their ears and leading them out of the kitchen, down the long drive and away from the farm. One poor dog-handler had to run to catch up and tripped over a walking stick with a dog's head that just happened to fall out of a coat stand as he was passing.

I nudged Thorn; I needed to know how this was happening. He clearly thought I was being infuriatingly human, but shrugged and waved his hand before my eyes and then the world looked very different.

How to explain? Well to begin with everything was transparent, as if someone had drawn too heavily with a pencil and then tried to rub it out and only a faint trace of the picture was left behind. I could see what the police were seeing. It was a kitchen, not a very tidy kitchen, but one that had everything a kitchen should have; but everything else, the things you wouldn't expect to see but were there; the hole in the wall, the tree reaching in and the cauldron sitting in the centre of the floor, were hidden behind or underneath the false kitchen. It was just plain sneaky! I remember thinking, so this is glamour, a trick to hide the truth, so much for being glamorous!

A man in a blue suit, not a uniform – so he must have been in charge – walked into the room. He looked around, picked up a dirty cup and dropped it on the floor; it didn't smash, so he stamped on it twice until it did. Then he walked across the room, until he stood by me, and looked out the window, that wasn't really there. He sighed as he looked at the garden that also wasn't there – it was Hill's bum he was looking at – then shook his head and began shouting; "That's enough! Everybody out! Seal off the whole area. We'll wait for the forensic squad. If their stash is here they'll find it. Have we heard from Detective Sims yet?" he asked one of the officers.

"No sir, they can't get hold of him."

"Can't get hold of him, you wait until I get hold of him," he scanned the room, squinted and growled, "this place is dodgy, I can feel it. Out! Everybody out!"

Three seconds later the house was empty – apart from me and five hundred or so Good Folk – who instantly began to celebrate, as only five hundred or so jolly Good Folk can!

"Silence!" the Crone shouted as she walked into the room, "how did this happen? How did these men come to stand on our threshold?"

Thorn stepped forward, "My lady, they were led here by Bottle."

"That's not true!"

"Are you sure of that?" she asked.

"Yes. Well… it's not exactly true," I protested.

"To be exact," Thorn continued after flashing an icy glare my way, "the money we gave Bottle, was used in one place. And more than once, so they discovered our imitations. This led them to Bottle and his father. Bottle's story of how he came by the money led them here."

The Crone changed into the young girl, "is this true Bottle?"

"No, it's not. Yes I guess, it is but it's not as bad as it sounds," all my energy and courage drained from me, Thorn was right, "yes, yes that's right."

"The contract is broken," Thorn hissed.

The girl changed back into the Crone and declared, "The contract is broken."

Thorn's hand grasped my chin. His flint blade pressed against my throat. I shut my eyes and wished I could say goodbye to Mum and Dad.

Chapter 24

There was silence and then a snigger and suddenly the whole room was laughing. Thorn released his grip. I opened my eyes, they weren't just laughing, they were rolling around roaring with laughter; they were bouncing off the walls and ceiling with laughter!

"What's going on?" seemed the sensible thing to ask.

The Crone changed into the beautiful woman who put her arm around my shoulder and gave me a firm squeeze, "Poor Bottle. Poor Bottle of the contract," again the whole company collapsed with laughter. The woman wiped the tears from her eyes and continued, "you have done well Bottle, better than some thought you could ever do."

I saw Thorn nod, "It is true."

"What have I done? I don't understand."

Thorn's hand rested on my shoulder, "You have shown your worth Bottle, you have shown courage and loyalty and honesty. You have demonstrated that you have a good heart, and we value that above all else… because we lack these things in ourselves."

I felt Fiddle poke my belly, "It's simple Bottle, don't look so worried, there was no contract… it was a ruse."

"A ruse, a trick?"

"Do we look like law makers to you?" Fiddle grinned, "contracts and such things are for men, not for the Good Folk. We live by bargain and barter but before you can do such things you must ensure both parties are to be trusted."

"We know we cannot be trusted, but you, we didn't know you at all. You could have been as untrustworthy as us," Thorn slapped me on the back and giggled, "so we had to find out."

"And we have Bottle, we have…with you we can bargain," the Crone said with another squeeze.

"But I knew all your names?" I garbled.

"A simple knowing spell."

"And the thing with the slate, all the spitting and the blood."

"That was so funny," Fiddle observed, "the look on your face."

I didn't think it was funny, I was furious, "my Mum's ill, she's dying, and you waste my time, sending me to do your shopping. Dragging me into this…nightmare, as a joke. What about this Green Man business I suppose that's nonsense too."

The Good Folk fell silent.

"Is he even real?"

"He was once, a long time ago," Nettle mumbled.

"I don't believe you…" but what was the point of getting angry, their ways, were not my ways. I'd wasted enough time on them. I'd been so caught up in things that I hadn't really thought about Mum and that made me feel awful. Dad had been at the police station all day, so Mum probably hadn't had any visitors all day. She was bound to be worried, or worse thought we'd abandoned her. My legs started shaking and if I hadn't sat down, I'm sure I would have fallen. Panic had me, I was full of fear. I wanted to run but couldn't move, I wanted to scream but couldn't find enough air to fill my lungs. I was sick and dizzy and felt trapped and furious.

Chapter 25

"And so, to the rescue plan," said Thorn, "Bottle and I struck a bargain, we shall keep our part and rescue your father."

"No you won't," I stated flatly, "I don't want your help."

"A deal is a deal Bottle. I suggest those of us that can pass unseen make their way into the stronghold and locate our man." Several hands were raised to volunteer. "Depending on the location, we have several options. We break in using a glamour, or we storm a wall, or if need be, the portcullis! Then we grab our man and run for Avalon. We'll give these men a fright they'll never forget!" There was a real murmur of excitement. "However," Thorn went on, and to make his point he sat on the ceiling, "I favour another option." The Good Folk fell silent, full of expectation. "We draw them out by creating such a stir they are forced to move their prisoner and then, as in the days of old, we waylay them. We then trap them, drive them wild with fear and then make good our escape."

This got a round of applause from all... except me.

I looked at the strange and wildly weird bunch of creatures that filled the kitchen. Wonderfully fantastically and strange, as different as different could be. And thought, maybe there's a reason these creatures have been hidden away in Avalon for so long, maybe we are better off without them, and maybe it's safer for them to hide away from us. Perhaps they belong back in Avalon away from the world of men that has turned them into myths.

"No," I said quietly.

"No? Why not? Do you have a better plan?"

"It's no good Thorn, it's no good. There's only one way to do this."

"Which is?"

"Let me tell you what's going to happen, I'm going to see my mum. The police will return with teams of men and crowbars and machines and they're going to take this place apart, and when they've done, they'll either board it up so no-one can get in, or knock the whole lot down. And I'm going to let them, because only then will they know my dad is telling the truth, I found the money here. And they'll let him go."

"And what about us?" said the Crone, turning into the little girl.

"I don't know. Hide as best you can, run away, and try to live with whatever's left behind; or move, retreat. The world of men and the world of Avalon just don't belong together. Find a Yew tree and get as far away from here as possible."

"But Bottle, we are all here to help you, we are here for you!" Nettle implored.

"I'm sorry I didn't find the Green Man. Tell the Apple Man I'm sorry about the crumble and the Birds custard."

The Tit sisters Blue, Coal, Great and Long-tailed squealed.

"No, it's not made out of… oh never mind. Goodbye," I walked out of the house, and I didn't look back. I knew what I had to do.

Chapter 26

I headed for the hospice, head down, arms pumping, focused on one thing, getting there. And then I heard steps behind me. Light, fast steps, but deliberate, as if the person wanted me to know they were there. I just kept going.

"These are the actions of a peeved child," Thorn growled, "they are not worthy of you."

"Go away Thorn, this is nothing to do with you."

"I said, I would help you free your father."

"That will take care of itself. I'm going to see Mum."

The footsteps behind me stalled, and then, restarted, "I shall accompany you."

"I don't want you there. Go away. I don't believe in fairies, I don't believe in fairies."

The footsteps stopped; I did not look back.

The Hospice was open twenty-four hours a day. There was a nurse on the reception desk I arrived, she greet me with a concern look; "We've been trying to get hold of your dad," she said, "the doctor's been with your Mum all morning. We tried to call you before, do you know how we can get hold of your dad?"

"I want to see the doctor, I can't get hold of my dad, I want to see my mum."

The nurse called the doctor over the intercom system, and the doctor: Dr Harriet Shaw, a nice lady with kind eyes arrived.

"We tried to call you," she stated, "do you know where your father is?"

"He's been arrested by the police. Can I see my mum?"

Dr Shaw's eyes widened, and then resumed their usual kind expression, "of course, but she lost consciousness two hours ago, she's very weak. It won't be long."

The nurse offered me her hand, "I'll go with you."

"No, I'm okay doing this alone, thanks."

The light above my Mum's bed hummed and shone directly onto her face but her eyes were shut tight, oblivious to the light. I took hold of her hand and squeezed, but she didn't squeeze back. It was strange, she looked comfortable, more comfortable than I'd seen her look for a very long time. I was glad of that, but I knew what it meant, she was leaving and there was nothing I could do... but of course there was. There beside her bed, was the apple of Avalon. I picked it up, it was still and firm and fresh. I almost heard Thorn's warning, 'there will be consequences,' ... but would it save her? Dr Apple keeps the day away... I didn't know what to believe.

"There will be consequences," Thorn growled coldly, from the other side of the bed.

"How did you get in here?" I demanded.

A thin ice crack of a grin split Thorn's face, as he handed me his flint blade, "the choice is yours Bottle."

"But what choice? What choice do I have?"

Thron shrugged, "only you know that, and you'll only know when you've chosen."

I grabbed his knife, cut the apple in half, and then cut a thin sliver from the centre of the apple and pressed it to Mum's lips; they were cold to the touch. I put my cheek to her lips, listening for a breath but heard nothing. I pressed the pulp into her mouth, but she did not chew. The juice ran from my fingers onto her lips, and she swallowed.

"Quickly," Thorn urged, "get her onto the floor, quickly, do it now Bottle, do it now!"

I grabbed hold of Mum's hand as Thorn pushed her off the bed, I caught her as best as I could, and laid her on the cold floor. Thorn then pushed the bed against the door and threw the bedside table on top of the bed.

"What are you doing in there? What's going on?" shouted Dr Shaw and the nurses, as they beat on the door.

"What's going to happen?"

Thorn grabbed hold of me, "that which is Avalon's stays in Avalon. Hold onto her, you must not be separated, if we lose her now all is lost. Hold on!"

I could feel a tremor, a slight rumbling and then the floor quivered and the walls groaned. Soon the whole room was shaking and each and every brick, tile and floorboard trembled and screamed; then suddenly a huge gnarled root exploded through the floor. Another broke through near my foot and then another beside Thorn and another and another until they completely surrounded us.

"What's happening Thorn?"

"Don't fight it. The apples of Avalon are claiming their own."

The roots wrapped around our hands and feet and then more and more broke through the floor, and coiled around our bodies, tighter and tighter. I saw roots cover my mum's face in a lace mask just before my own eyes were blindfolded by Avalon's roots. I held my breath; and then the world of mud swallowed us whole.

Chapter 27

I came to with Hill slapping my back and roaring at me to; "Breathe Bottle! Breathe!" – which I was doing.

"Please put me down Hill, drop!" I was dropped.

I was standing within the stone circle, whilst Thorn and the Apple Man were busy piling up a mound of earth at its very centre. I pushed them aside and saw my mum buried up to her face in dirt; I freaked out and started swinging punches at all of them, but Hill caught me up and held me tight. The Apple Man spoke gently to me; "be still Bottle be still, she has been through much, and was close to the door of passing, it will take some time but she will be well."

Hill dropped me again, and I fell to my knees, my face to my mum's face; my tears turning the dirt to streaks of mud across her cheeks.

"She will be well," the Apple Man assured me.

"Can I stay with her?" I asked.

"I'm afraid we have more pressing problems," said Thorn sounding like he had the weight of the world on his shoulders, "bring him in."

Nettle, Dock and Bog marched into the circle, they were escorting a bound figure - "Dad!"

He did not answer. He didn't even look at me.

"There was a bit of a misunderstanding," Nettle mumbled into his own leaves.

"What happened?" I asked with my heart sinking.

"Well, you know you said, go rescue my dad, go rescue my dad and I will be forever grateful."

"I did not say that."

"No, well that's what we wanted to hear, so that's what we heard, so that's what we did."

I looked at my dad's blank expression, "what happened?"

"He swallowed a frog of forgetfulness," Bog burped, "I wouldn't worry. It should wear off. It usually wears off. It should have worn off already... but it was a big frog... it could possibly have been two. Things got a bit wild, what with the chase through the town and all."

"The chase?"

"The issue is," Thorn asserted, "your omen of foreboding has proved to be true. The police are at our gates. They have brought many men and many machines."

I raced back over Haggis Hop, through the kitchen and out through the entrance hall; to see that Thorn wasn't kidding; in fact, he was downplaying the situation. The space between the gate and the farmhouse, where the long spooky drive should have been, was now a dark foreboding muddy expanse covered with a shining veneer of slime. Beyond it, just outside the five-bar gate, were six police patrol cars, their flashing blue lights sending stars out across the dingy swamp; and behind them another six vans, a JCB excavator, and a caterpillar tracked crane with a huge stone wrecking-ball; with at least twenty figures in white overalls milling around in-between them. And somewhere up above, far out of sight, I swear I could hear a helicopter hovering about.

"Where did the swamp come from?" I heard myself say.

"That not a swamp, that's a lake of the purest crystal-clear glistening water. A gift from Sulis," Bog burped, "she really is awfully sorry about what happened."

"I wonder what they want?" Nettle mused.

"Want?" I exclaimed. "Really? They want us."

"Typical greedy interfering humans," Thorn growled, "it's always been this way, ever since they believed that nonsense about us having hordes of gold and silver."

"No thorn," I growled back, "they want you for forgery."

"You see, it's always the same with these humans, gold and money, it's always the same," Thron declared haughtily.

"And…" I wasn't going to let him get away with that, "we just destroyed half a hospice. Kidnapped a dying woman, and if that's not bad enough; you broke into a police station and rescued the suspected forger, and then…" I took a deep breath, and ploughed on, "and then, you lead them here, to the very place they think is at the heart of the forgery ring; which it is!"

"It's a tricky one, I'll give you that," Nettle pondered sagely.

"For a bush you're incredibly dense," I huffed, "what are we going to do? That mud won't keep them out for long."

"We fight," Thorn growled drawing his flint blade.

"And then what…" the Crone's voice cracked dryly behind us, "you think they'll stop coming because you beat them, because they've seen what you can do, seen who you are? They'll never stop, more will come."

"What do you suggest we do then, hide?" said Thorn, withering slightly as he spoke, "there's too many of them to fool with a glamour."

"Everything has its time," the Crone's voice wavered, "come in and shut the door. We have preparations to make."

We followed the Crone back into the wreck of a kitchen, where she spoke softly and soothingly to all that were gathered there, quivering their wings and shaking their leaves. "Children, dear ones, brothers and sisters, all things must pass, and we have lingered long in the world of men. Perhaps too long. It is time to abandon the light, and return to the darkness under the hill," the Crone turned into the beautiful woman that the Apple Man had called Morgana and began giving orders in a clear bright voice, "Thorn, take charge of the cauldron, take it to the edge of the chasm, and hold it there for as long as you dare. Little ones go forth and spread the word, all those that dally will be lost, we return to the earth, Avalon is fallen." She then turned to me and laid a hand on my shoulder. "I am sorry Bottle, the Apple Man will stay with your mother for as long as he can, but if she does not rise before the cauldron falls. I cannot say what will become of her. You and your father should leave while you can, I suspect he'll come to his senses… eventually."

"Wait a minute, what about Doctor Apple and Avalon looking after its own," I protested.

"My dear Bottle, did you not hear, Avalon is fallen," a tear welled in her eye, "we must leave the land of Albion and be no more."

"I'll stall them," I heard myself say, "I'll give you time to get everybody out, but you must take my mum, you must promise to take my mum."

"If she leaves with us, you'll never see her again," the Crone replied as she melted into the little girl.

"If she stays, I've already lost her. I'll buy you some time… I'll do something, just don't leave her behind," I stated, not having any idea what I was going to do.

I stepped out the front door, closed it behind me and walked to the edge of the muddy expanse. My thoughts were easy to gather they went like this: "What are you doing? What are you doing? What am I doing?" I felt very alone and yes, I was afraid, but I knew whatever I was about to do, I had to give it my all.

The man I'd seen earlier that day, smashing the cup in the farmhouse kitchen, stood in the arc of the flashing blue police lights and walked through the gate, "Kay, isn't it?" he shouted.

I was, so I nodded.

"Go find your father and bring him out."

I shook my head.

"Kid, my name is Critch, I'm not a police officer. I'm the National Crime Agency, I work for the Crown, the head of state you understand? We deal with forgery, we prosecute fraudsters like your father, for the Crown. We tell the police what to do, and they do it, so you tell your dad to come out here now," he took another step forward, and pointed to the farmhouse, "because when we get started, we're going to knock down every wall and brick until we find where and how your dad forged that money. And when we've done that, we're going to level the place, just to make sure. If your dad is in there, he's going to get hurt. Tell him to turn himself in now."

My mouth was dry with fear, I couldn't speak. I wanted to rage and scream at him to go away, to tell he was going to ruin my only chance to save my mum and drive away all that was marvelous and magic in the world – that I did believe in fairies, and he was going to end it all; but I couldn't say a word, I just stood there shaking.

The man raised his arm. The JCB's engine roared, "last chance."

I balled my fists and gritted my teeth, "you'll have to go through me first."

The man laughed, and the JCB rolled forward, crushing Lone Farm's five-bar gate to pieces. The police cars and vans followed in its path; with the white clad officers forming an advancing line across the muddy drive.

"Grab the boy," Critch shouted, "don't let him get away."

The wreaking-ball brought up the rear, its long arm immediately caught in the overhanging branches, snapping them like twigs. Critch marched towards it, ordered the driver from the cab and climbed aboard. The machine's tracks clanked, bit into the earth and rolled forward. Critch blasted a warning on the machine's horn as the wrecking-ball dropped. The vehicle's body spun back and forth, launching the ball forward into a tree, smashing it to splinters. Critch cheered and moved onto the next one. As the wrecking-ball was busy tearing up the trees, the JCB was tearing through the muddy lake as if it wasn't there; picking up speed it sped towards me. It was ten feet away when I heard a loud crack and a split appeared in the ground a few feet from where I stood. The muddy water flooded into the gap, I lost my footing in the rush, and landed in the mud on my back. The JCB couldn't have seen me there, covered in mud, because he picked up speed, and drove on – and then the JCB seemed to jolt, hop to one side, and then rose up on a wave of undulating mud. The driver just had time to jump clear before the excavator disappeared into the earth. The split in the ground near my feet burst open and Dug, Dig and Ditch came piling out.

"Sorry Bottle!" Dug panted, "we tried to stop him!"

"We're sorry," Dig wept, "we didn't mean none of it! It's not our fault, he's too strong!"

"Run Bottle run!" yelled Ditch, "he's coming!"

The ground shook, men faltered and fell, and the sky darkened. Moments later the clouds opened, and the sky was ripped by lightning. Dug, Dig and Ditch ran to me, and we huddled together in the mud, as the storm raged about us. Lightning struck the Yew tree to my left, smashing it to flaming pieces. Smoke stung my eyes and pelting rain peppered my face; but through it all, I saw something in the mud rise and stand, something broad, tall and strong. I watched as the rain washed away the grime to reveal; a big, strong man with long white bedraggled hair falling across his silver armour and grey chainmail.

As the other workmen fled the field, Critch drove on. The caterpillar wreaking ball belched exhaust and ground on towards the farmhouse; towards us - its ball swinging. Lightening streaked across the sky, illuminating the battered silver armour of the white-haired man as he stepped between us and the charging machine.

The mud at his feet swirled, rose, twisted into a spike and fell away; and there stood Sulis, her red hair burning like fire, her face glowing with light and joy. She bowed to the white-haired man and offered him a huge silver sword; she spoke a single word; "Excalibur."

The King took his sword, raised it high above his head, and charged the dragon.

In the flashing lightning I saw steel clash, spark and burn, I saw Critch thrown from the cab, and the King sever the swinging head of his monstrous foe. I saw the victor climb upon the dragon's writhing neck, and with his burning blade held high, ride its body down into the dark depths of the good earth. The rain fell and the sky fell silent.

"Bottle isn't it?" Sulis grinned down at me sweetly, "I'm so very sorry about the earlier misunderstanding. If there's anything I can do to right the wrong, I would be much obliged."

"Well..." I pointed to the men who were crawling through the mud and fallen trees, "I don't want to hurt anybody either but... they are ... Romans."

"Romans!" Sulis hissed.

"It would be best if they forgot all about us."

"Forgot... yes, I think we can manage that," she winked and then, with great dignity called, "Bog! Where are you Bog? Bog! Unleash the frogs."

Chapter 28

I left Dug, Dig and Ditch to assist Bog and Sulis in their work and returned to the farmhouse. The Good Folk may have been cheering, the Crone may have kissed my cheek, and Fiddle may have ruffled my hair; but I was not paying attention. I pushed my way through the crowded corridor, ran through the kitchen, and out into the yard that lead to Haggis Hop. And there was Thorn, the black cauldron in one hand, his flint knife in the other.

"You can bring that back in, they've gone."

He was so surprised he nearly dropped the cauldron, "what happened?"

"Avalon won... at least for now. Bring that thing in before you drop it you silly elf."

I made my way to the stone circle, but the Apple Man and my mum were gone; standing next to the recently dug hole, looking as perplexed as a person can be was, "Dad."

"Kay, where are we? What happened? I can't remember how we got here. I was at the police station and then... are you okay?"

I put my arms around him, and squeezed, "I'm okay Dad, but there's something I need to tell you." It was time to tell the truth, so I told it all, and Dad just stood there dumbfounded, until my truth telling was done; "… and that is how we got here, and I'm sorry I got you into so much trouble, and I'm sorry I lied about the money and the Good Folk and … well there it is."

"Kay fairies aren't real, whatever you think you've done, whatever you think has happened, you need to realise that you've been under a lot of stress, and I'm sorry, I'm sorry I didn't see it but…"

"Dad. Believe me fairies are real, but that's not the point, the point is, I got us into this mess."

"No Kay," Dad insisted, "you didn't, and fairies aren't real. I don't believe in fairies; you don't believe in fairies."

"You don't believe in fairies! You don't believe in fairies!" screamed Fiddle, as he reeled into the stone circle, spun on his pin thin legs and fell to the ground, twitching at my father's feet, "say it isn't so milkman, say it isn't so."

"I do believe in fairies! I do believe in fairies!" Hill roared, clapping his hands wildly as he jumped into the stone circle.

The laughter that followed would have awoken Pendragon again, if it were possible to wake him; as the Good Folk rushed into the circle, picked us both up and ran us around and around the stone circle until I felt decidedly dizzy.

"Give heed, give heed," the Crone called out as they set me on my feet, "to you Bottle we give thanks this Beltane Day. You have been our guide and you have brought us our greatest wish. Welcome, welcome home, Green Man." And there they were bowing to my dad.

"Hold on a minute," I protested but my words were lost in another cheer, as a parade of flower fairies fluttered into the circle and began circling around my dad.

The Crone bowed, the Good Folk bowed, one and all, to the flower covered figure that now stood before my father.

"Mum?"

It was Mum, but her hair was longer, and her skin was younger, and lavender blue. She looked at me and smiled, but it wasn't the smile of recognition, not the smile a mother gives to her child; she didn't know who I was.

"My Queen," the bowing Crone turned into Morgana, and bowed even lower, "let me introduce you to the hero of the hour, Bottle."

"Bottle, yes," my mother beamed, "I am told we have much to thank you for, you have found the Green Man, we are most grateful."

"What is this? What have you done?" I shouted.

"Jean is that you?" Dad stared, totally transfixed, "what happen to your hair?"

Mum smiled, stroked his face with her hand, and with the other, offered him an apple.

"Dad don't!"

"Join me in Avalon beloved, eat of Avalon and be of Avalon forever."

It wasn't fair, it wasn't right. He didn't know what he was doing, he wasn't thinking straight, how could he be? His sick wife was young again and offering him an apple, of course he took a bite.

"We give thanks to Bottle for bringing us a new May Queen and our new Green Man. Hale and hearty is the Queen of the May!" cheered the Crone.

"What have you done?"

The Crone placed her hand on my shoulder, "we have brought to lovers together, we have given hope, where there was none."

"You tricked me."

"How so?" Thorn's icy fingers gripped the back of my neck, "I warned you Bottle. I told you there would be consequences; you can't say I didn't."

"I trusted you Thorn, I trusted you."

Thorn threw his head back and laughed, "no you didn't, that just isn't true. And if you did; what were you thinking? I'm a silly elf. We told you we needed a Green Man, and you brought us a man and his bride. The May Queen is restored, and they shall live Bottle, long happy lives, they shall live. Tell me how we tricked you?" he snorted and wandered back to the party.

I fled from the stone circle and sat on the edge of the chasm, my head buried in my hands, my eyes full of tears, and my head full of fear; what would become of me? I think I must have worn myself out with rage and crying, because I almost fell asleep – and almost fell, tottering forward into the chasm, when a voice called; "Have a care there Bottle, it's a long way down," it was Mum, draped in silk and flowers, "I'm told the return journey is fraught with danger, including a Jack and Jill and their fearsome bucket."

"I think you might be remembering that story wrong. You used to read me that story, do you remember?"

She smiled sweetly, "I can't say I do."

"Are you still my mum?"

"I am the Queen of the May … you were once called Kay, and I was Mum, and you were my son."

"Our son," Dad's ever cheerful voice broke in, "nothing can ever change that, even though everything else has changed, that remains."

"Will you stay with us awhile Bottle," my mother smiled, "we can never leave, but you can come and go as you wish. The world beyond Avalon needs such as you, those with a good stout heart and the courage to use it."

"Stay and let us get to know you Bottle," my Green Man father said.

"Yes, stay and get to know us Bottle," Mum smiled.

Epilogue

Anyway, that was all a very long time ago. Times have changed and although time changes slowly within Avalon it does still change. The May Queen and her Green Man reigned happily for many years, and they proved to be just what the Good Folk needed; even when the Good Folk didn't want them to be, they were what they needed them to be, good parents.

The Good Folk need good people around them, just like everybody else does, it just makes life easier. They're looking again you know, looking for another King and Queen.

Which brings us to the end of my tale, I hope you enjoyed it and maybe even learnt a thing or two about those pesky folk who live in the shadows, but just one more point if I may, if you remember anything about this story, remember this; If you ever do see a fairy or a talking walking stick, just keep your eyes open and your wits about you, and remember be careful… our ways are not your ways.

The End

Neil S. Reddy

Writer of short stories and fiction published in **but clearly doesn't know a fing about the Good Folk! this is our story not his and he's not Bottle and Bottle should never had told him. They'll be trouble!**

JP Lawrence

Independent illustrator working in a number of media and genres, he lives in Basingstoke England **and didn't do a bad job really, although Fiddle say his nose isn't that big and why didn't he draw me? has he got something against Nettles... yes that's right I can type too!**

THE GOOD FOLK

RULE O.K!

Dank House Manor